MW01286521

DIRTY LITTLE SECRET

FORBIDDEN DESIRES–BOOK ONE

KENDALL RYAN

Dirty Little Secret

Copyright © 2017 Kendall Ryan

Copy Editing and Formatting by Pam Berehulke

Cover Design by Okay Creations

About the Book

Gavin Kingsley burst into my life in a sharp and unexpected twist of fate. You know his type—arrogant, dangerously handsome, and impossible to ignore.

Something dark within him calls to the shadows inside me. I long for the kind of heart-wrenching passion I've only read about, and his tragic past reads like one of my favorite literary classics. Raw. Visceral. Captivating. Together, we're a perfect mess.

The deeper I fall into his world, the more I crave him like a drug—he pushes every boundary I have, and challenges everything I thought I wanted. I want to unlock his heart. I want his dirty secrets.

But in the end, will he be the blade that cuts me . . . or the bond that makes my life complete?

Written in the same vein as Kendall Ryan's New York Times bestselling and much-loved international phenomenon, *Filthy Beautiful Lies*, *Dirty Little Secret* begins an erotic new series.

Prologue

Dirty secrets. We all have them. We guard them fiercely, protecting them like a mother does a precious newborn infant, cradled to her chest, away from the world's prying eyes. Yet those dark, forbidden desires we crave won't stay hidden for long. They have a way of coming out—usually at the most inopportune time.

I knew all that, and yet . . . I watched them from a distance, knowing they'd be perfect together. They were two halves of the same whole. He was broken beyond repair. She was so familiar, reminding him of something he desperately wanted to fix. I knew she'd be perfect for him.

In the end, the chain of events this would to set off would be fucking massive, yet I was powerless to stop it. Instead, I was there in the middle of it all, stoking the flames and praying they didn't take me down with them.

Chapter One

Emma

My entire morning revolved around this thirty-second encounter. And if I timed it poorly and missed it? My whole day would be shit.

I needed it like a shot of adrenaline to start the day.

Every morning, careful to make sure my makeup was perfect and my hair was in place, I'd stop at the coffee shop on my way to work. I'd linger, staring at the rows of gourmet pastries and handcrafted mugs.

And every morning, promptly at ten to eight, Mr. Tall, Dark, and Sinful strolled inside and ordered a double shot of espresso to go.

Our routine had gone unchanged for the last ten months, and even though I cherished every second of our time together, we'd never spoken a single word. Hadn't even made eye contact. For all I knew, he thought I was one of the commuters grabbing a mug of something hot and strong on my way to work. Just like him, I assumed. Or worse, maybe he didn't even notice I existed.

Until one morning, I'd stepped into line behind him and, for some inexplicable reason, he'd turned and looked deep into my eyes. I couldn't say how long the eye contact went on, probably only a fraction of a second. But even so, I felt like my lungs would collapse from the weight of his hazel stare boring into mine.

Since then, I'd tried a few times to recreate the moment, to wear some new perfume that might catch his attention, or pull my brown hair into a different style that might catch his eye. But nothing had made a difference. No, I was certain he didn't even know I existed. Which was for the best, since I was pretty sure this was borderline stalking.

But then, that had been before everything changed. It was the precursor to something that would alter my life forever. Something that would make everything richer and sweeter and deeper . . . only to have it all fall apart, leaving me to piece together the shattered fragments.

Luckily for me, though, every instant was etched perfectly into my memory, even now as I struggled to decide if it felt more like a curse or a gift.

That morning, the scent of roasting coffee beans had

filled the air, and steam formed inside the windows from the warmer-than-usual foggy September day.

I was standing in the corner, admiring the new array of teas for the fall, when the door chimed behind me, forcing me to turn around and look for the man I knew would be there.

He was dressed in his charcoal-gray suit—one of my favorites. The fine material stretched across his sculpted biceps and wide shoulders enticingly. His crisp dress shirt was navy, contrasted by his silver tie. Every inch of him was polished. But it was the scowl painted on his chiseled features that made my knees weak.

In the months since I'd first seen him, I'd imagined a life for him, even come up with a few names and rough ideas of what his office and apartment might be like. I never saw what he drove, but I was certain it must be something fast and sleek.

As for his job, I was sure he had a high-powered career as a corporate attorney or a stockbroker, or maybe a real estate investor. Something where he was in control, and his powerful body and almost overwhelming presence could do most of his talking for him.

"Espresso—" he said, his voice rough but sensual, deep and intoxicating. I'd often imagined the way my name would sound rolling off his tongue.

"Double shot, to go," the barista finished for him, smiling.

It seemed I wasn't the only one who had him pegged. The man was nothing if not predictable.

He gave her a curt nod, his gaze drifting to the smartphone in his hand that had just let out a demanding ping. From where I stood a few feet from him, I glanced over, trying to get a peek at the background of his screen to see if there was a picture of him with a woman, or maybe one of a child set as his screensaver, but no. Just the standard factory presets.

He was all business. There was little fanfare, no *good morning* or other greeting to the staff at the café, not even a friendly smile. But that voice, though . . . pure sin.

I swallowed hard and stepped in line behind him, thinking of it now as he stood inches from me. If I introduced myself, I might get him to say my name, another moment to carry with me late at night when I lay awake thinking of him with my hand down the front of my panties.

Instead, the barista set the cardboard cup down in front of him. He handed her a black matte credit card, waiting with his hand outstretched as she swiped it.

Almost as if in slow motion, he turned. Shooting a look over one broad shoulder and holding my gaze, he dropped something into the glass jar in front of the register. Then he grabbed his coffee cup and strolled away like nothing had happened.

And for a second, nothing did.

"Nice tip, asshole," the pink-haired barista muttered as the door chimed closed behind him. She plucked a business card from the tip jar that was otherwise filled with crinkled dollar bills and coins, then tossed it into the trash can behind her before ringing up my order for a small tea.

I waited, staring at the discarded rectangle as a sense of panic washed through me.

Maybe it was because I was standing on the cusp of thirty, or because I was suddenly single for the first time in forever. Maybe it was because the possibility of ending up as a sad cat lady now seemed like a very real possibility. Whatever the reason, I did something reckless.

My heart pounded out an unsteady rhythm as I reached toward the barista. "C-can I see that card?" Totally pathetic and I knew it, but I couldn't help myself.

She eyed where it rested on the top of the trash can—seemingly stuck to the side of that morning's new trash bag—and then looked back at me.

"Please," I added, letting a hint of my desperation show.

Rolling her eyes, she picked up the card, brushed off a few errant coffee grounds, and extended it toward me. "No skin off my ass."

I plucked the card from her fingertips and muttered an apology, unable to help the fact that I was acting like a crazy person.

The heavyweight linen card felt sumptuous in my hand. Rubbing my fingers across the raised ink, I couldn't help but wonder if he'd left this on purpose. If he'd meant for me to find it.

He didn't strike me as a careless man, didn't seem the type to make the mistake of dropping his card where he meant to leave cash. As weird as it sounded, that look, the way he'd held my gaze? I was sure this was deliberate. I felt it in my bones.

Before I could even process my destination, my black ballet flats were carrying me toward the door.

"Miss," the barista called after me. "Your tea!"

I rushed back and dropped some money on the counter, then told her to keep it and waved a hand in her direction before continuing toward the door.

I didn't need the tea. I'd gotten what I came for.

Clutching the card, I rushed down Second Avenue, oblivious to the people rushing past me. I made it to the bus stop just in time to see the hulking, dusty city bus squeal to a stop. After trudging up the steps, I found a seat in the front, the card still in my shaking fingers.

I lived in the heart of the city, even though I couldn't afford it, even though I worked thirty minutes away in the suburbs. There was something romantic about living downtown—the history of the buildings, the quaint brownstone I lived in with its charming front steps, built over a hundred years ago. Nothing about living in an apartment complex with concrete strip malls decorating the landscape appealed to me. Well, nothing except the idea of a functioning kitchen and a modern bathroom bigger than a coffin, but hey. A girl couldn't have everything.

A rush of nerves settled in the pit of my stomach at the thought of my house. At this point, I wasn't even sure I could afford to keep it, never mind remodel, but thinking about it only made my heart ache. It had been my grandmother's, and the memories I had there couldn't be replaced.

I shoved aside the harsh light of reality and settled back into my fantasy world.

For the next few minutes, I let myself daydream. Would his name be something masculine and old-fashioned, like Jack or Michael? Or maybe something unexpected, like Finn or Ansel? I'd waited for this moment for so long, I made myself slow down and savor it.

By the time I pushed my way through the front doors

of the library, I was almost trembling with excitement to find out. I slowed as I entered the foyer, stopping to wave to Stan, the library's technical assistant. He was a nice guy, but it grossed me out how he brought the periodicals into the men's room with him.

Slowing down briefly to flick on the overhead fluorescent lights, I continued behind the counter and down the short hallway that led to my office. I swung open the frosted glass door with EMMA BELL, HEAD LIBRARIAN emblazoned across it in gold and black, and rushed in with a sigh.

Mrs. Duncan retired last year after spending forty years as the head librarian, and now the job was mine. I loved it, loved everything about this sleepy library, but in this moment, the last thing on my mind was work.

Shutting the heavy oak door behind me, I let out a shaky breath and sank down into my stiff wooden chair. Opening my palm, I revealed the card and the little indents where the corners of the paper had pressed into my skin.

My lips twitched into a smile as I finally allowed myself to read what it said.

Gavin Kingsley

President

Forbidden Desires

Gavin.

My fake boyfriend's name was Gavin, and it was freaking perfect. My smile widened. A hot name for a hot man.

There was no contact information, no phone number, not even an email address, which was . . . strange. Not that I would have contacted him. God, what would I say? *"Hi, I'm the mousy brunette librarian who stares at you at the coffee shop."*

No, thanks. His rejection was one humiliation I'd rather forgo.

But, wait.

What was Forbidden Desires? It was apparently a company he ran or owned. Swirling my mouse across the mouse pad to wake my laptop, I typed FORBIDDEN

DESIRES into the search engine and waited while the outdated machine slowly populated the results.

A lot of questionable websites came up, so it took me a few tries to locate the correct one. But when I did, I still didn't think it could be right. Not really. Yet the photo of him there was undeniable.

My mouth fell open and I stared at his image, so chiseled and handsome. And just like that? All my theories about him being a corporate ladder climber died on the vine. Because Gavin Kingsley, whoever he was, was into something a whole lot more sinister.

"Emma?"

My pulse hammering, I quickly closed the browser and turned. Bethany was smirking in my office doorway, her slender arms crisscrossing her thin frame.

"Sorry. I didn't mean to interrupt." She raised her palms in front of her. "You look like you just saw a ghost."

I shook my head, willing myself to calm down. "No worries. You just startled me. What's up?"

"We have a ten o'clock field trip coming in, and then

an author reading in the Steinbeck Room at eleven. Do you know how many people we're expecting? I just want to make sure we're ready."

I flipped through the stack of folders on my desk and handed her the one that read SPECIAL EVENTS across the top. "Here you go."

"Thanks." She smiled. "And you might want to grab the Lysol. Stan just went into the bathroom with a stack of reading material again."

I nodded and cringed. "On it."

Bethany was in charge of marketing and public outreach, and we'd become good friends in the last six months. We occasionally got together on the weekends, meeting up for dinner or to try a new yoga class.

All of that had transpired more recently. Or, as I was now calling this era in my life, PN.

Post-Nathan. Maybe I should rebrand that, though. Call it something like NE—New-Emma— to put a more positive spin on it.

But I wasn't new. I was just finally able to be myself for the first time in a long time.

Blinking, I tried to force myself not to think about the time before now, or what I might call that.

The Dark Ages.

The Bad Times.

The Emotional Upside Down.

I did the things my therapist had told me not to do. I thought of how I should have known better, should have seen the abuse coming from a mile away. How I should have walked away when I first realized how Nathan isolated me from my friends and family. How I'd lost three years believing he loved me, thinking he would change.

It was painful, even now, so many months later, but I reminded myself of what my therapist had said. My family had forgiven me and were happy to have me back. I was making new friends. My life was on track.

Now all I had to do was forgive myself and move on.

But if what I'd seen online was any indication, I still had no reason to trust myself, especially when it came to men. Gavin Kingsley was clearly trouble. Maybe if I researched him more, though, I'd find his situation was different from what it appeared.

Maybe . . .

"Emma! Code Brown!" Bethany shouted from down the hall, and I sat up a little straighter.

Shoving my thoughts away, I rose from my desk and followed her into the hall, armed with my trusty bottle of air freshener and disinfectant. As much as I wanted to keep reading about Gavin, I had to focus on work, and then tonight? I would look at the website again and find out exactly what kind of man I was dealing with.

To my surprise, it didn't take long to get Gavin off my mind. Between the absence of my head children's librarian on field trip day and three readings, I found myself trudging toward my bus stop at the end of the day in what felt like record time.

And when I got home? I had two things on my mind: a nice hot bath and Gavin Kingsley.

• • •

Sinking into a bubble bath that was almost too hot, I released a sharp breath.

I'd wanted to unwind, give myself a chance to relax before I revisited the website, but even thinking about it made my shoulders tense.

On the ABOUT US page, there hadn't been much information, just a picture of three men, all of whom looked relatively similar in that they were stunningly attractive with bright, inquisitive eyes. Gavin stood in the middle, his smile a little less warm and open than that of the others.

I closed my eyes, thinking of the way he'd dropped his card into the jar at the coffee shop.

It had been on purpose. There was no doubt.

He'd wanted someone—maybe me?—to know the truth. That he was the president of what appeared to be a rather kinky dating site.

I still couldn't wrap my head around it. All these months, I'd fantasized about him being some sexy attorney or investor, not a man involved in something so depraved.

From what I could gather on the website, it wasn't a sleazy operation where money exchanged hands for sex. It was more upscale than that—a *CEO needs a date for a charity gala* type of thing.

But, still. It was called Forbidden Desires. Surely some secret fantasies were being acted out. Surely it wasn't all innocent. It reeked of rich, powerful men who got what they wanted, and took it by force when necessary.

My skin broke out into goose bumps despite the warm water.

Inhaling a deep, calming breath through my nostrils, I lifted my favorite novel from its resting place beside the tub, opened the worn pages, and pushed the swirling thoughts from my brain.

My damp fingers soothed the deep crease on the dog-eared page as my eyes skimmed the words. I nearly knew the whole thing by heart.

I love you as certain dark things are to be loved, in secret, between the shadow and the soul. Pablo Neruda's "Sonnet XVII" was a favorite, and his words slid through me like a knife through softened butter.

After reading a few pages but not absorbing much, I

stepped from the tub and toweled off. My mind was still firmly on that silky business card I'd nabbed earlier.

My old house was drafty and cold, so I wrapped myself in a plush floor-length robe before wandering to the kitchen to pour myself a glass of chocolate milk from the carton in the fridge.

Simply wishing I had the courage to take a leap wasn't going to change my situation. The only thing that could change the course of my destiny was action.

And as scared as I was, I was more scared not to try . . . more scared of never knowing what the man behind those piercing hazel eyes was like.

Grabbing my phone from the counter, I opened the website that had taunted me all day, hovering my finger over the screen.

With the information I'd already uncovered, I should be afraid. I should run the other way—throw away his business card and erase him from my memory. But I couldn't bring myself to do it, so I did the one thing I knew I shouldn't.

I took a deep breath and clicked the CONTACT US

icon.

Chapter Two

Gavin

"Alyssa? Can you get your ass in here?" *Fuck.* "Please?"

I smirked at myself, proud that I'd asked nicely this time. She'd given me hell last week, said she was tired of the way I barked orders through the intercom all day.

She was the best executive assistant in the city of Boston, and didn't hesitate to let me know when I was out of line, which was often. I couldn't risk her deserting me. So, like it or not, I needed to mind my manners now and again.

"Mr. Kingsley." Alyssa raised her eyebrows as she entered my office and stopped beside my desk. "You rang?"

I met her gaze and held out a single sheet of paper.

"Our newest client is Troy Drake." When she simply leveled me with a blank stare, I prompted, "Tech CEO, and cousin to the billionaire entrepreneur Colton Drake?"

She shook her head. "I'm not familiar."

"Doesn't matter. My point is that he's an important client."

Her light eyes flashed with understanding and she nodded, making her black ponytail swing behind her narrow face. "Of course, sir. I'm happy to pair him with whichever woman he desires."

"Good." I released a heavy sigh. Not that I'd expected Alyssa to put up a fight. She might not have been regularly obedient, but she knew when things counted, and this client definitely did.

Troy Drake had already given me a fat deposit, and I wanted him happy. He'd just recently moved to the East Coast, said he didn't know anyone yet. Plus, he was wealthy beyond belief, with deep pockets and even deeper connections. If we made him a satisfied client, I had a feeling he'd not only stay with us for years to come, but would also refer his colleagues our way.

Not that we were desperate for business—quite the opposite, actually. After five years in business, my brothers and I were now clearing eight figures annually, and the upside was limitless. But being from the wrong side of the tracks and building our wealth from nothing bred a constant hunger for more. We could never allow ourselves to get too comfortable or to lose focus.

As Alyssa stepped away from my desk, I held up my hand, silently asking her to stay put.

"What's the problem?" she asked, more than a little familiar with my mannerisms by now.

I pinched the bridge of my nose between two fingers and met her narrowed gaze again. "He's been through the database, and no one struck his fancy."

Alyssa blinked twice. "No one?"

Our girls were top notch. I should know; I'd sampled a few of them myself. But this guy was young, attractive, and loaded, and he certainly wasn't desperate for a date. He had come to us because he wanted something special. Something discreet. A sure thing.

And I wanted to provide it. It was kind of my thing. I'd never met a client I couldn't turn into a satisfied customer, and had never met a woman I couldn't bed. I didn't want things to change now, not right when I was on the cusp of something great.

"I have an idea," Alyssa said, grinning like she knew

something I didn't. "I may have someone in mind, actually. There's a new girl here for an interview with Sonja right now. She could be perfect. Articulate. Demure. Very pretty."

I nodded. "Perfect. Send her in when they're through."

Alyssa paused but nodded all the same. I didn't often interview the girls myself, but I had a special interest in keeping this client happy. She left, closing the heavy mahogany door behind her, and I turned my attention back to my in-box.

A few seconds later, the door opened again and my younger brother, Cooper, strolled into my office with his hands in his pockets and an easy grin on his face.

"Hey," he said, either not noticing or not caring that I hadn't invited him in and was clearly busy.

Annoyed, I glared at him. "What do you want, Cooper?"

He chuckled and slid into the leather chair across from me. "Nice way to greet me, asshole. I just wanted to tell you the corporate quarterly tax payment is going to be slightly higher than we projected. But not to worry, we have the funds to cover it."

"And why is it going to be higher than anticipated?"

He shrugged. "We're making more money than expected. It's a good thing."

I waited, knowing Cooper was about to crack a joke or tell me about his latest exploit with one of the girls. It was his afternoon ritual, despite the fact that he knew it annoyed me. Though, to be fair, half my annoyance had to do with the fact that Cooper, six years younger than me, still had that playful quality those of us past thirty seemed to lose.

My intercom buzzed again.

"Mr. Kingsley?" Alyssa's crisp voice blared over the speaker. "A Miss Emma Bell is finished with Sonja. Shall I send her in?"

Who? Oh, right. Probably the potential escort for Mr. Drake.

"Send her in."

When Cooper shot me a questioning glance, I shook my head. "You can stay. This should just take a minute."

The door opened, and in walked five and a half feet of luscious curves and a body built for sin balanced precariously on a pair of black stilettos. My cock gave a twitch, eager to say hello.

Finally, I lifted my gaze to her face, and all the breath left my lungs in a whoosh.

It was the girl from the coffee shop.

What the fuck is she doing here?

She was a classic girl-next-door type. A walking wet dream. Someone I had no right to desire, but I wanted all the same.

I could have ended this a long time ago, could have chosen a different coffee shop, could have used that overpriced espresso machine sitting on my kitchen counter, yet I'd done none of those things. And instead of putting her out of my mind, I'd left my business card on a whim, hoping she'd miss my cue or ignore it.

And perversely hoping she wouldn't.

Now, here she was, and I felt like I'd been kicked in the chest. We'd been building to this moment for too long—something had to give. And damn if it wasn't sexy the way she'd taken matters into her own hands. It was ballsy, and I couldn't deny it. I was intrigued.

I glanced at her, looking for recognition in her eyes, but if she knew we'd met before, she certainly didn't show it. Instead, her hands were clasped patiently in front of her, forcing her cleavage together in a perfect little vee as she stared past me blankly.

Was it just an act, the same way I'd pretended not to notice her every morning at the coffee shop had been? Or was she toying with me?

All my senses were humming, on high alert, and I was more interested in something than I'd been in a long time. Energy buzzed in the air around us, and I took a moment to compose myself.

Chewing on her lower lip, she stopped in front of my desk.

"Miss Bell?" I asked, snapping out her name curtly.

She gave me a tight nod, her eyes not yet daring to meet mine.

"Gavin Kingsley, and this is my younger brother, Cooper."

Her eyes locked with mine at last, and my gut clenched at the determination blazing in that steely sapphire gaze.

"Sit down." I hadn't intended the command to come out so briskly, but it had, and she immediately lowered herself into the seat across from me and beside Cooper. With another surge, my cock swelled again at her willingness to obey my commands.

Down, boy.

"What brings you to Forbidden Desires today?" I asked, my voice cool.

She opened her mouth to speak, but when only a soft whimper came out, she cleared her throat to start again.

If she was going to act like we didn't know each other, far be it from me to spoil her ruse.

"Would you like something to drink?" I asked with a smile.

"No, thank you."

It was the first time I'd ever heard her voice outside of her usual order. It was a potent combination of feminine and sweet, one that had once brought me to my knees.

"Tea, perhaps?" I couldn't help the smirk tugging at my lips as I waited to see if she'd react to that.

She shook her head, though by the way her eyes flashed, I knew the joke hadn't escaped her. "I'm fine."

"Then please enlighten us." I gestured for her to go ahead.

Cooper's eyes narrowed, and I knew what he was thinking. *Why the fuck are you being such a dick?*

"Sir?" she asked, her gaze confused as she tried to understand what I wanted from her.

"Why are you here at Forbidden Desires, Miss Bell?"

"I was ... intrigued. By your website." She paused again, weighing her words. "I thought I'd come in and see what you had to offer."

About nine inches of hard—

I cleared my throat and cut that thought short. Leaning forward, I placed my palms flat on my desk. "I'm sorry, but I'm not buying it. A beautiful woman like yourself, what could you possibly be doing here?"

"I—"

"You need money, is that it?"

Her eyes narrowed. "No, nothing like that." Her attention flicked to Cooper, whose narrowed gaze was still trained on me.

"What then?" I pressed. "What is it that you're looking for?"

Watching me intently for several more seconds, she drew a steadying breath that made her nostrils flare slightly. She seemed to be gathering her inner strength.

"Adventure."

She hurled the word with enough force to tell me that this one had spirit. There was the backbone I'd been wondering about.

This was ridiculous. I was sure that my clients—including Drake—would eat this woman for breakfast.

It was exactly that thought that made me want to usher her right out the door. Since the second she'd walked in, one realization had become clear. I couldn't have her. I wanted her too much. Giving in to a clawing need like this would ruin us both. That much I knew from experience. But for some strange reason, the thought of anyone else having her made my hands clench into fists.

Leaving my card had been a grave error on my part. I'd gotten cocky, thought I could handle it, but I was dead wrong. Now to get her out of my sight before I couldn't resist the urges that were stirring deep inside.

"Sorry, but I can't help you." I rose from my desk and she mirrored my stance, rising to her feet on shaky heels.

"Surely, that's your job, Mr. Kingsley," she said softly. "To cater to people's . . . desires?"

Our tense standoff stretched out for several seconds, during which Emma refused to back down and my cock twitched in interest yet again.

Fuck.

I had too much to lose now, too many people counting on me. She was a distraction. And in my line of work, she was one I couldn't afford. I needed her gone.

"Certain dark things are meant to be explored in

secret, don't you think?" she asked, her voice gaining confidence. When my gaze flitted to hers, a smile unfurled on her lips.

"One point on which we well agree, Miss Bell."

Even as the warning bells blared in my head, I couldn't seem to force myself to make her go.

Chapter Three

Emma

Holy hell.

Gavin Kingsley was the most intense, arrogant, and infuriating man I'd ever met. I didn't know whether to stomp out of his office or to curse him out. But I was raised better than that, so I sat there with my lips pursed, watching him, waiting to see what he'd do or say next. So far, he'd been anything but what I'd expected.

His intense gaze held mine, holding me captive. The weight of his stare was much too sensual, almost as if . . . as if it were his calloused fingertips grazing my bare skin. Blood rushed to my cheeks, and to certain other parts of my body, against my will.

Both he and his brother appeared smug, like all of this was familiar territory for them and they were used to getting their way. They were both dashingly handsome, of course, each over six feet tall, well-muscled and broad. Gavin's square jaw was dusted with yesterday's stubble, and his hazel eyes drilled into me so intently, it was hard not to gasp. While Gavin's suit was impeccably tailored, his tie still knotted neatly at his throat, Cooper's tie hung loosely about his neck. The younger brother had ditched his coat somewhere, and the sleeves of his once-crisp white shirt were rolled up to his elbows, exposing strong, tanned forearms.

So similar in some ways, but totally different in others.

I hadn't figured them out, not by a long shot, but it didn't matter. My time here was done.

The men made eye contact over my head, seeming to communicate something I wasn't privy to.

Gavin's lips pulled into a slant as he looked back at me again. "If you're here looking for love, if you think you're going to find it, that's not what we do here."

What had I been hoping to find?

That he'd recognize me and declare his undying devotion? Or maybe leap up and take me in his arms? Tell me he'd been waiting for me for so long?

What an idiot I'd been. Instead, he'd leered at my breasts for a second and then made a joke about my morning tea, the only indication that he recognized me at all.

Gavin wasn't a fantasy. He was a nightmare.

Shame poured over me, forcing heat to rush to my cheeks. "It was obviously a mistake to come here. Excuse me."

Real life was not some romance novel. In fact, this moment seemed to belong to the horror genre, or maybe even dark comedy, depending on your outlook. Either way, I wouldn't subject myself to his patronizing questions any longer.

"One second," Cooper said, stepping between us. "Give us just a minute, would you, princess?"

I met his gaze and wet my lower lip with the tip of my tongue. The term of endearment coming from his mouth was tender and unexpected. He had kind eyes, and in that moment, for some strange reason I trusted him, much more than I probably should.

"Okay," I said.

Cooper escorted me to the door, and when we stepped into the hall, he muttered under his breath, "He's being a prick."

"Is that unusual?" Maybe this was just the way Gavin operated. All I had to go on was viewing him in a coffee shop. I knew nothing of the man, but so far, this didn't seem all that out of character.

Rather than answer, Cooper frowned. "Give me two minutes with him. We'll sort this out."

Heaving a sigh, I stood my ground. "One minute."

"You won't leave? I know you said it's not about the money, but I have a great idea that could benefit us all, and we pay well. Very well," he said, his voice softer than I would have imagined for such a big man.

"I'll wait," I said, although I fisted my hands at my sides in self-disgust. I had no reason to stay. In less than five minutes, I had been insulted in more ways than I could count by a man I knew was my type—which made things all the worse. But the thought of being able to pay off what I owed on the brownstone and get ahead a little was tempting.

Almost as tempting as getting inside enigmatic Gavin Kingsley's head and figuring out what the hell he was thinking. It was a curse. The same quality that made me a great researcher and a dedicated librarian also made me almost tragically curious. I couldn't stand a puzzle unsolved, and Gavin was definitely that.

Cooper went back inside the office and closed the door behind him with a soft click, leaving me to wonder what exactly they were discussing, since the general topic was obviously me.

I should have left. Every part of me knew it, and my whole body vibrated with the desire to run . . . except one tiny part that I couldn't seem to quiet. The ember burning deep in the pit of my stomach that kept me rooted to the spot.

The one that told me if I stayed, everything would change. That the adventure I'd been longing for waited just on the other side of that door.

Chapter Four

Cooper

This was so fucking amusing.

I'd never seen Gavin get so worked up over a girl before, let alone an escort, not even when he'd been with . . . well, not in a long damn time. To him, each one was pretty much interchangeable with the last. Yet this one was beautiful, feisty, and had him all riled up. I could have laughed, if it weren't for the intense rush of blood engorging my cock.

Who could blame me? Emma Bell was stunning. Sexy, but subtly so. Confident, but with a hint of shyness that was as hot as fuck. And even odder still, she seemed to have no idea what she was doing here. Which, I supposed, made three of us.

I was sure there was a story here, and damn if I didn't want to uncover it, but first things first. I had to deal with Gavin.

As soon as I reentered the room, careful to close the door behind me, Gavin launched into speech.

"She's not right for this company, Coop. She's—"

"I agree with you. She's not the type to sleep around." I held up one hand, wandering toward the windows to appreciate the city view below. I could feel his eyes on my back; he was surely wondering what the hell I was up to. After a moment of silence, I asked, "But I have one question. Who are you taking to the charity auction?"

"What? What does that have to do with anything right now?"

I knew he expected me to ask why he was being so hostile. Which, of course, meant I couldn't. Not yet. If he was expecting the question, he'd never give the answer.

I shrugged. "Emma could be the perfect companion, don't you think?" I turned to face his desk, where he still sat.

He rolled his eyes, and I swooped in for the kill. He'd had his chance. I'd given it to him on a silver platter. Which meant that the coast was clear. If he didn't want her . . .

"So, you don't mind if I take her to the Bennett Foundation gala?" I raised my eyebrows.

Gavin's brow furrowed but his eyes went ice cold, his pause saying far more than his words. "Of course not. Why would I mind?"

Bullshit.

Maybe this little push was just what he needed to get his head out of his ass.

I nodded. "Good."

His mouth turned down a notch, and I could tell he was thinking. Processing.

For a moment, I didn't think he was going to take the bait. But then, I knew my brother. I'd laid down a challenge, questioned why he was so adamantly against the idea of hiring her, and although he didn't want to open up and share, this topic was far from over. Our calendars were slammed, and we both knew it. His assistant had joked just that morning that it would make her job a hell of a lot easier if we each just got a girlfriend. Gavin had scoffed so hard, I thought he was going to bust an artery.

Gavin heaved out a sharp exhale. "What makes you so interested in her, anyway? I thought they were all a number on a paycheck to you?"

I shrugged. "They are until they're not. You, of all people, should know—"

"Enough," Gavin barked.

"Right." I shoved my hands in my pockets. "Shame, though. Seems like there's something . . . interesting between you two." Briefly, I wondered if they had a history. "Anything you want to tell me?"

"No, but I have a question for you," he snapped back with a lethal smile that didn't reach his narrowed eyes. "What the fuck are you still doing in my office?"

"Trying to find out whether you're going to let me have this one, or if we're going to be fighting for the same prize," I answered honestly.

Gavin looked up from his screen. "Are you high?" His mouth thinned into a firm, chiseled line. "If you want her, take her. I'm not playing with her like she's a chew toy."

"Okay. But that doesn't change the fact that you need a date to the charity auction. A girl like her on your arm? Imagine the business we could do. She's like a walking commercial. And when you're done rubbing elbows with all the fancy people, I'll take her off your hands for a couple of events of my own. Use your head, man, she's perfect. The girl every guy wants to be seen with. Sweet enough to bring home to Mother, hot enough to imagine her on her knees, with that mouth—"

"Got it," Gavin snapped. He stared at a point on the ceiling, then blew out an annoyed sigh. "If I take her to the fucking auction, will you stop, already?"

"Yup."

"I'll tell you right now, though, if this is business, neither of us are sleeping with her."

I bit back a laugh but nodded anyway. If that was what Gavin wanted to tell himself, I wasn't about to stop him. Fact was, though, if she would have either of us, we'd probably get our dicks caught in our zippers in the rush to get our pants off. Telling him that would only make him change his mind, and I'd gotten what I wanted.

If this girl had my big brother this riled up? She was something special. And no matter what he thought of himself, he deserved something special in his life again. If I had to agree to take her out as well just to get him to go along with it, so be it.

It wasn't exactly a hardship, after all.

Gavin turned his attention back to his laptop, ignoring me and signaling that the conversation was over. If he wanted me to believe he didn't care about the beautiful creature whose scent still lingered between us, he almost had me fooled.

Almost.

But I'd known him too long. He never let a woman affect him, and this one evoked a response from him that I hadn't seen in a long time. It was dangerous, but I believed Gavin had learned his lesson the hard way. The past needed to stay there. Emma could be a fresh start.

"May the best man win." I stepped around his desk and clapped him on the back, and Gavin's frown deepened.

"This is not a contest," he ground out.

"Sure, it's not." I chuckled. It was an outright pissing match, and something told me it was going to be damn amusing watching Gavin lose his cool when I won her over.

I went out of the office and ushered a confused and nervous-looking Emma back inside, then closed the door behind us.

"Sorry about that, Emma. Please, have a seat."

She did, lowering herself into the chair once again, this time with a demure smile. I certainly had better manners than my beast of a brother, and Emma, for one, appreciated them.

One point for Cooper.

Only once she was seated did Gavin's attention lift from his laptop.

"If we do this," I began, "enter into this arrangement with you via the company, things will be different from our usual contract with our escorts."

"Different, how?" Emma asked, looking between us.

Gavin cut in. "What did Sonja tell you about how the agency works?"

Emma crossed one slender leg over the other, and her hesitant gaze flitted up to his. "That the clients of your firm are professionals, often CEOs and professional athletes who need tasteful dates who are both beautiful and discreet and often available on short notice."

She'd gotten the gist. The escorts were also paid handsomely—the average going rate was about a thousand bucks for an evening.

"Good. What else?" I asked.

Her cheeks flushed and her gaze dipped to her shiny black pumps. "She told me about the blood tests and medical exam, though she stressed that sexual relations are not part of the deal and totally up to the escort and the client, but that sometimes it does happen."

"That's true, as well," I added.

Gavin's smirk made me want to knee him in the balls. Damn desk was in the way, though.

"You'll have to excuse my brother," I said. "He's like a naughty preschooler who can't share his toys."

The crease between Emma's brows told me she didn't miss the reference to being one of our toys.

"What he means to say," Gavin said, looking exasperated, "is that rather than have you work as an agency girl, we feel we could keep you busy just between the two of us."

Emma's pretty mouth pulled into a frown.

Goddamn it. Gavin was about as smooth as a sheet of sandpaper.

"As owners of the company and heavily involved in the day-to-day operations, we have little time for dating, or visiting local establishments to pick up women. You understand," I said. "And we're always looking to drum up new business. What better way to do it than to be seen with one of our girls?"

Emma nodded hesitantly, her pink cheeks going a little pale. "That makes sense."

"I have a charity gala later this week, and Gavin has an event the week after. We thought perhaps . . ."

"I see. So, just us three." Her voice wavered as she looked between us.

I smiled. "Exactly." *Just us three.*

My goal was to put her at ease, but two rich, powerful men sat before her asking her to essentially date us both. Of course, this was all new to her. The pulse in her neck strummed hard and fast and yet she remained willing, at least, to hear us out.

"Can I think it over?" she asked.

"This is a surprise, I'm sure. Of course you can," I said.

I half expected Gavin to cut in and tell her the offer expired in twenty-four hours, or something equally ridiculous, but fortunately, he did no such thing.

"The girls who work for us are treated very well," I told her, "and I'd be happy to refer you to any of them if you want more information. We have nothing to hide."

Emma nodded, and then we all rose to our feet. Gavin shot me a warning glare, but I grinned back at him with a wink.

Game on, bro.

In my head, though, I was seriously rooting for my brother. He'd been in such a dark place for so long. The thought of him stepping back into the light, seeing him smile a little more?

Man, I'd give almost anything for that. Maybe pretty little Emma Bell could be that light.

But in my heart? There was a part of me that hoped I was wrong. That maybe he'd find sunshine somewhere else.

Because I could use a little sunshine too, and for some strange reason, Emma Bell made me feel warm from the inside out.

Chapter Five

Emma

What a disaster.

I hadn't meant to sign up for their agency. I'd merely wanted to go to Gavin's office to see if I might catch a glimpse of him, to ease a little of the burning curiosity I'd had since finding his business card. Now, I couldn't recall exactly because it was all a blur, but I was pretty sure I'd agreed to prostitute myself out to a pair of brothers who owned an escort company.

Good grief!

When I'd arrived and the woman at the front desk assumed I was there for an interview, I hadn't corrected her, I'd just followed her inside her office and answered her questions politely. Admittedly, I'd been curious about Forbidden Desires, and was eager for a glimpse into the company that Gavin ran.

The meeting with Sonja went by in a blur. She was polite and discreet. It was almost as though she was interviewing me for a secretarial position.

And then I'd been so nervous when she ushered me into Gavin's office, I'd barely been able to string together a coherent sentence in front of him and his brother.

I'd nodded along with what they said, waiting until I got outside the building to let a string of curse words rip. I'd just have to call them back in the morning and let them know there was no way in hell I could ever go through with something like this.

The two of them together were overwhelming. So much masculine energy, the room practically overflowed with testosterone, making me dizzy. They were each over six feet tall, and where Gavin was dark and handsome with a chiseled jaw dusted in dark stubble and piercing hazel eyes, Cooper was lighter with messy golden hair, green eyes, and a playful grin.

But Gavin . . .

I couldn't quite put my finger on it, but his demeanor and harsh words seemed to bypass my brain, charging straight into that secret part of me I always kept firmly hidden. The part of me that wanted to be cherished and worshipped, to please a man so deeply I knew without a doubt was my other half.

I'd left with a promise to call tomorrow and give Sonja my response to their proposition. Too bad I wasn't entirely sure what that proposition was. Did they really just want someone on their arm for a couple of events? Or did they expect me to sleep with them?

I shivered at the thought, recalling the way Gavin's gaze moved over my body, leaving a trail of flames in its path. As I made my way home on the number seventeen bus, I let out a panicked chuckle and pushed the thought—and the Kingsley brothers—from my mind, forcing myself to contemplate what to do with my evening. On my phone, I placed an order for Mediterranean take-out food and mentally calculated how many episodes I had left to watch of my favorite show on Netflix.

Back at home, I changed from my black pencil skirt and cream silk blouse into yoga pants and a sweatshirt. Then I proceeded to gorge myself on falafel and shawarma, promising I'd hit the gym extra hard in the morning.

Only after my pre-bedtime routine, while wrapped up in a blanket on my couch with a book in my lap, did I allow my mind to wander back to the day's events.

Gavin had been totally unlike I'd expected. He was cold, almost rude. I realized now that my expectations had been based on pure fantasy. A fantasy that was better left to my dreams at night.

I pushed my glasses higher on the bridge of my nose and tried to shove him from my brain. He was nice to look at, but I was done with men who treated me like I was merely an afterthought. It was foolish, but I wanted the kind of love I read about in the pages of my favorite romantic literature. I wanted a man who worshipped and adored me. My very own Heathcliff, without the dramatic ending, of course.

And Cooper? He was different. I knew he would be sweet and kind . . .

But he was still a man who was looking for a date with an escort. And that meant he had no interest in something real.

Talk about delusional, Emma.

Releasing a heavy sigh, I willed my gaze to focus on the words on the page and ignore the discontent stewing inside me. But now that my mind had started to wander, it was intent on taking stock of how lonely I'd become in the ten months post-Nathan ... and even long before that, if I was being honest with myself.

This was how I ended my days—alone in my brownstone, one of my favorite literary classics in my lap, my glasses pushed up high on the bridge of my nose.

Getting up to pour myself a glass of my favorite nightly treat, the chocolate milk I kept in the door of the fridge, I realized my life hadn't always been like this.

Back when I was with Nathan, when it had all started out, I'd thought it was going to be a typical relationship. Girl meets boy; girl falls in love. And all that did happen, but it wasn't that simple.

We were set up by a mutual friend, and everything was fine for a while. I never could have imagined it would turn into such an ugly, abusive relationship.

Before Nathan, I was confident, strong-willed, and knew right from wrong. I wasn't a pushover. But slowly, as he burrowed deeper and deeper into my life, he began to manipulate me, taking me down a very, very dark path.

My waking hours were spent worrying over what he

might do, what he might say about a decision I'd made. He had opinions on everything, from my job and my friends to my wardrobe and how I spent my paycheck.

Slowly, Nathan began to isolate me from my friends and family, making it so I was reliant only on him. The scariest thing was that I didn't realize any of it was happening. It was a gradual fall.

And then? I woke up two years later with a swollen, puffy red eye and knew I had to leave, or one day he would quite literally kill me. My self-esteem was at an all-time low, and I knew I needed to make a drastic change.

I took a gulp of my drink, dumping the rest down the drain as an unexpected sharp knock at the door startled me.

Pursing my lips, I tossed on my fluffy pink robe and ventured to the peephole to look out. No one was there. When I opened the door, I found a large round black box resting at my feet, a pretty silver bow affixed to the top. Looking up, I watched a uniformed messenger climb into a delivery van in front of my house.

With trembling fingers, I lifted the box and carried it

inside to my dining table, tugging the white note that was affixed to the top of it. In elegant, bold script, there were three words staring back at me.

For you.

— Cooper

Again, I had that tingling sense that everything was about to change.

And suddenly it made me angry.

Yes, I'd harbored a secret crush on Gavin for the better part of a year—but it was a dream, a wishful thought. In my imagination, he was untouchable, and therefore a safe option to fantasize about. The reality of him and his *interests* was a little too grim for my liking.

I'd made my decision the second I left his offices in the glittery tower. I might have been intrigued, but that was as far as it went. I told Cooper I'd consider their offer, and for just a moment, I had.

But even my determination not to get involved with

these men didn't stop me from opening the box. It was as though my fingers moved of their own volition, pulling open the lacquered lid carefully until I saw what was inside.

Holding my breath, I pushed aside the mounds of crisp tissue paper, then lifted the gown from its resting place inside, admiring the feel of it in my hands. The glittery gold fabric was surprisingly heavy with fine boning and delicate glass beads painstakingly sewn into the sheath bodice.

I let out an indignant snort. I'd be returning this ridiculous gown.

Right after I tried it on . . . just once.

And who could blame me? I'd never worn a gown this exquisite in my life. I'd never had a reason to.

The ring of my cell phone in the other room captured my attention, and I marched out to retrieve it. The only people who called me were my mom and Bethany. The number on the screen was one I didn't recognize.

"Hello?"

"Miss Bell," a deep, slightly familiar voice said.

"Who is this?"

"Cooper Kingsley. Did you receive the dress?"

"Oh yes, I did, but—"

"You didn't like it?"

"It's not that, it's just . . ."

"It didn't fit?"

His tone remained smooth and steady while I grew increasingly flustered. I took a moment to compose myself, drawing a deep breath into my lungs.

"I've put some more thought into your proposal."

"I see. Well, I don't think it would be fair to discuss this without Gavin. Why don't you come into the office tomorrow and give us your answer? Good evening, Miss Bell." And with that, he clicked off.

I was left staring down at my phone, my heart thrumming steadily. Apparently, giving him a piece of my mind would have to wait until tomorrow.

Chapter Six

Gavin

"Another invitation," Alyssa said, handing me a stack of mail. A thick black envelope was perched on top, its crisp top edge having already been sliced open by her letter opener.

"That one's for A Way Out?"

She nodded.

Slowly, I slipped the invitation from its black casing and ran my fingers over the raised silver lettering. I attended the gala each year, and the invitation always looked the same, complete with the feminine silhouette along the edge of the paper.

I fingered the RSVP slip and sighed at the little blank space meant for me to enter how many people would be in my party.

"They'll be expecting me," I said. It was more to myself than Alyssa, but from the corner of my eye, I saw her nod.

And, of course she did. Because she knew, like I did,

that it wasn't just a regular charity event, not just some chance to show off our girls and pique the interest of our fellow wealthy CEOs.

For me, A Way Out was personal in a way that had nothing to do with the job. Some people considered our company a short hop to prostitution, but that was far from true. We certainly didn't condone it, especially not in the way that so many people viewed it—preying on young naive girls, getting them hooked on drugs and the like. Our girls were smart, driven, and knew exactly what they were doing. More importantly, though, none of them were expected to sleep with the client, and that wasn't PR. That was a fact.

And when it came to human trafficking? We actively fought against it, just like this charity did. They embraced our patronage with open arms because they knew that our business was merely a glorified dating service—we hooked up CEOs, celebrities, and politicians with dates for high-profile functions.

I wasn't naive enough to believe these liaisons never ended in sex. Of course they did, but the girls set a steep price outside of our regular fee and that money was theirs—we'd never take a cut. We were a registered business, paid our taxes, and donated time and money to a variety of good causes.

It was all very much on the up-and-up.

Those were the things I had to remind myself of late at night. When sleep wouldn't come, and I lay there thinking of the times when things weren't within my control. Back when it wasn't always in my power to fix everything. Back when things had gone so horribly wrong. And in the darkness of my bedroom, a twinge of guilt, a sense that I needed to do more to end the nastiness that existed out there, would hang over me like a swarm of bees.

It didn't trouble Quinn or Cooper. Prostitution was the oldest profession in history, and they thought we could make it safer for the girls if they chose to do it, but we couldn't stop it. No matter how much we wanted to. They didn't blame me for what had happened, but that didn't absolve me of anything. I knew who'd been at fault.

"Will you be needing a date, sir?" Alyssa was still standing in front of my desk, no doubt waiting for me to dismiss her.

Sliding the invitation from its resting place, I glanced down and shook my head. "I've got it covered. Thanks, Alyssa. You may go."

I watched her exit the room, thinking of last year's event. She'd gone with me, as I'd felt it was important to showcase the female staff of the business, and had been by my side during the cocktail hour and auction.

With her encouragement, I'd bid on and won a weeklong vacation on a private island off the coast of South America, or was it Australia? I couldn't remember. I still didn't know what I was going to do with the damn thing. Quinn had been pressuring me to go for a while now, to get away from it all, but there was no way I could walk away from the job for more than a day or two at a time. There was too much to do, always too much, and this wasn't a nine-to-five business. I was in the office six or seven days a week. And without me being here? I had no way of knowing everything was in control.

Fifteen minutes later, I'd answered a few emails and read over Cooper's latest proposal, finishing just in time for my intercom to buzz.

Alyssa's cool tones floated over the speaker. "Sir,

Miss Bell is here to see you."

I tapped my fingers restlessly on my desktop as I let that sink in. So, she had come back for more. Probably to tell us to go to hell, but still . . .

Despite the increase in my pulse rate, I kept my reply short and easy. "Send her in."

Alyssa hesitated, the intercom system blinking at me. "Shall I notify Cooper as well?"

I glanced at the place where Emma had sat across from me yesterday, so prim and proper. Waiting for my instruction.

I should call him in. I could use the buffer. Instead, I said, "No. I'll handle it myself."

The intercom flickered off and, in the space of an instant, my heavy mahogany door swung open and Emma walked into the room, her pretty bow of a mouth set into a determined line.

She looked different today. It wasn't her outward appearance—she was dressed similarly in pressed black pants, a cream silk top, ballet flats, and those little spectacles pushed high on her nose that completed the sexy-librarian vibe. The difference today was in her attitude. Her shoulders were thrust back, her chin lifted, and her eyes blazed with a soft confidence that I found . . . what was the word?

Captivating.

"Close the door behind you," I said, my tone more brusque than I'd intended.

Emma glanced at me as if on the brink of arguing but then obeyed, letting the door fall closed before approaching my desk.

"Thank you for coming in. Please, have a seat." I gestured to the chair behind her.

"I'd rather stand. I won't be here long." A delicate hand came to rest on her hip, and I couldn't help but smirk.

Was this her attempt at intimidation? If it was, I couldn't help but wonder where she'd learned it. Or if it had ever, even once, been effective. Because from where I was sitting, it just made her look equally adorable and fuckable. I shifted in my chair in an attempt to alleviate the sudden pressure against my zipper.

"All right. Tell me what's on your mind." I clasped my hands in front of me on the heavy stainless-steel-and-glass desktop.

She glanced at my hands, and then her gaze met mine. The confidence, however faint, flickered for a moment, but then her nostrils flared. "I've given it more thought, and I'm sorry but I'm not interested in this . . . arrangement with you and your brother."

Perfect. It was for the best across the board, really.

But that wasn't what I said. I looked down and adjusted the dial on my wristwatch, taking a moment to pause before I replied. "I don't believe you."

For a guy who needed to be in control all the time, I seemed to have no control over my actions around her. I should take this out she'd given me. Step back before I got in too deep.

Her petulant mouth fell open into an *O* before she caught herself and pressed her full lips together. Drawing a steadying breath, she started again. "I've made up my mind, Mr. Kingsley, and I find your tone rude and derogatory. If you'll excuse me, I'll be going now."

Honestly, I could have laughed. I knew something she didn't. I knew this interaction ended with her unequivocal acceptance.

I waited until she turned, only because I wanted another glimpse of her sexy ass. It was a fine, ripe thing ready for my hands and my mouth. But that would have to wait. Just like last time, all rational thought had fled under the heat of the chemistry that sparked between us like a Fourth of July fireworks display, and suddenly, letting her walk out of here again seemed like a crime.

Which meant it was time to play dirty.

"Miss Bell, we've already RSVP'd for your first event. It's a five-thousand-dollar-per-plate charity dinner benefitting international women's literary programs."

"I don't know why you went and did that. I didn't agree to this arrangement, precisely. I said I would th—"

"You realize, of course, that your library is running a night class that needs funding, is it not?" I raised my eyebrows.

Slowly, she turned, sweeping the tip of her pretty pink tongue over her bottom lip. "I never mentioned my job."

"But you did sign the waiver for the background check." I shrugged. "Complete with a record of your employment history. Come now, Emma. You probably do need the money, after all."

She paused, halting where she stood. "Money isn't worth sacrificing my dignity for."

"Maybe not." Reaching into the desk drawer, I produced the crisp check that I'd already written out that would go to the cause regardless. Then I set it on my desk. "But I'll provide a ten-thousand-dollar donation to that poor little underfunded library you work at. Is your dignity still worth more than that?"

She wandered a step closer. "All of this just to go to a dinner with you?"

We both knew this was so much more than dinner. Cooper and I were letting her into our world. Not just as a hired escort at Forbidden Desires, but as the personal mistress to us both. I didn't like showing my hand, didn't want her knowing just how badly I suddenly needed her to say yes, but desperate times and all that shit.

"Of course, that wouldn't be all," I added hastily, then pulled up a form on my computer. "It looks like you filled out the direct-deposit form, so you will be all set up to receive your compensation as well."

"Which is?" She raised her eyebrows, her tone light but curious all the same.

"Just like all the other girls. A thousand dollars a night."

"No way. That's absurd."

That steely gaze of hers was back, but her mouth was pinched into a little frown, considering. I hadn't lost her completely, no matter how much she wanted to pretend otherwise.

"We're paying for your time. Surely your time, and *dignity*, are worth something, Miss Bell? No money will exchange hands, if that makes you uncomfortable. It'll be deposited into your account. Non-negotiable."

"I . . ."

"Isn't there anything you could use that money for? A new car, maybe? A nicer house?"

Something in her expression told me I'd hit a nerve. In an instant, her chin lifted.

"Fine," she said, the fire returning to her eyes. "I'll go."

Her mouth knotted into a tiny circle. She crossed her arms over her chest, apparently trying to rally what little spirit she had left. "For the record, I'm not having sex with either one of you."

"Fine by me," I said. "For the record? I didn't ask you to. And further, it's not my business what you do with Cooper, but no, I don't plan on taking you to bed."

Her blue eyes flared on mine, and I couldn't tell if she was irritated or maybe intrigued by that comment. Didn't matter. I'd known from her glances at the coffee shop. She wanted me. And she would have me. I'd soak up that sensuality, take what I wanted, and when it was over, I'd be totally fine. Because I was strong enough to resist her. I couldn't get tangled up with another agency girl again. I knew my limits.

What happened last time had nearly destroyed me, my brothers, and this company. And that searing pain inside my chest whenever I thought of *her* was another reason not to drag the sweet, innocent librarian through a dark, dangerous adventure.

Not when it could cost us both everything.

But, surely, I was strong enough for a little fun. A flirtation. Something to quench my thirst for this woman.

Besides, there was no question I was a selfish bastard. If I didn't play along with Coop's silly little game, he would make a full-court press for this girl, and the thought of her in his arms and not mine? Made me want to put my fist through a wall.

"I suspect you have work to be done. Good-bye, Mr. Kingsley."

She spun on her heel again, but I caught her just as she was about to sweep through the door.

"Call me Gavin." My tone was biting, and I took a deep breath, trying to clear my head. I'd won today's argument, so why was I still so worked up? Gazing into her crystal-blue eyes, I worked to soften my tone. "I have a meeting in twenty minutes I need to prepare for, but thank you for coming in. Enjoy your evening with

Cooper."

She nodded, her eyelashes fluttering softly against her cheeks. And then she turned, flashing that curvy ass at me as she strode from my office. *Goddamn tease.*

My fingers returned to the keyboard and I continued typing out my reply, but my brain? It was still on a certain sassy young librarian who pushed every one of my buttons.

She was all wrong for me. Innocent where I was hardened, and sweet where I was rough. She'd want a tender lover, someone who was gentle and took his time warming her up, not some asshole who'd shove all nine inches in just to watch her gasp and struggle for breath. My cock flexed behind my zipper at the thought.

Cooper was the much better choice for her. So, why had I let him talk me into this arrangement?

It wasn't because I was a fucking moron who thought with his cock. That was Quinn, not me. I exercised control in all things.

It was because I saw the challenge in Cooper's eyes. Knew he thought she was too much like Ashley. Maybe she was—Christ, they could have passed for cousins. Maybe even sisters. And the need to prove him wrong, to show him that I could keep my head on straight, was too strong. Almost as strong as the desire to see Emma naked, spread-eagle on my bed.

I don't plan on taking you to bed.

I could have barked out a laugh if I wasn't so pissed off. What an utter lie. Of course I'd take her to bed. And as for what she did with Cooper? Why should I care? That was their business.

Punching the intercom button with more force than necessary, I waited until Alyssa's voice came through the speaker.

"You need something?"

"Bring me some seltzer water," I growled.

Damn knot in my stomach came out of nowhere.

Chapter Seven

Emma

Pink or red?

I stared down at the tubes of liquid lip stain I'd picked up at the department store on my lunch break. A classic bold red and a flattering girly pink. I usually opted for a swipe of nude lip balm, preferring the natural look, but the elegant gown I'd be wearing tonight called for something a little different.

Red, it is.

It turned out applying red lipstick precisely was a more difficult task than I'd been prepared for. Ten minutes later, I had blotted and reapplied until I was satisfied, leaving myself just enough time to step into my nicest pair of heels as my cell phone chimed with a text.

Cooper was here.

I forced a smile at my reflection, fighting the urge to curl up in my bed and pretend I wasn't home. Tonight was good for the library, and I couldn't back out now. And then, tomorrow? A thousand dollars would go a long way toward restoring this old brownstone to the way it had been when I was younger.

With a few dates, I might be able to put in an old butcher-block table and countertops like my grandmother had once had. I could plant a blueberry bush in the back. I might even be able to find an old rocker like the one she'd kept near the bay window. And a tub ... a humongous soaking tub.

I just had to think of those things whenever times got tough. On the bright side, at least this date was with Cooper and not Gavin.

My stomach flipped at the thought of it, and our last encounter. Why did Gavin throw me off my game so completely? He was just a man. Not some demi-god toying with the rest of us sad little mortals, which for some reason it always felt like. And I was pretty sure he knew it.

Which meant next time, I had to do better. Because, screw him.

For tonight, though, it was only Cooper and me, and everything was going to be fine. I just had to think of it as a normal date.

Still, the second things got weird or I felt disrespected, I was out of there. I wanted to keep this place, but there were some lines I wouldn't cross no matter what.

Grabbing my black envelope clutch, I tucked the lipstick and my cell phone inside and met Cooper on my cracked concrete stoop.

He was taller than I remembered, maybe even a little taller than Gavin, and looked striking in his tailored black tuxedo.

His gaze slid down the length of my body, his lips curving into a wide smile.

So, maybe he made no bones about his attraction to me. To this point, he'd never done or said anything inappropriate and had been a perfect gentleman.

Give him a chance.

"It fits," I murmured, gesturing at the ethereal concoction of a dress he'd sent.

"Perfectly." His voice was husky and his green eyes danced with mischief. "You are stunning."

I offered him a smile before accepting his outstretched hand and allowed him to help me navigate the stairs in my stiletto heels. His skin was warm and smooth, and his hand was so large, it enclosed mine completely. I felt a little bubbling in my heart like sweet champagne. And just like that, all my fears fizzled away.

He made me feel comfortable. Safe. Being with Cooper was easy.

Besides, maybe being spoiled and desired by two wealthy CEOs wasn't the worst thing that could have happened to me. And considering how nice and down-to-earth Cooper seemed, did I really have that much room to complain?

Relaxed and allowing myself to get a little excited, I climbed into the limo that would take us to the event.

"Something to drink?" Cooper gestured to the minibar, which was stocked with miniature bottles of liquor, sparkling water, and wine.

I shook my head. "I think I'll just wait until we get there."

"Good idea." He nodded, treating me to another

warm smile. "It's only a ten-minute ride to the venue. Have I mentioned how gorgeous you look? I feel like I really can't put too fine a point on it."

I grinned, then gazed out the window, taking in the view as the city passed by in a blur. My life didn't involve limousine rides through the city, or expensive gowns or galas. That was the stuff of *Cinderella* and *Pride and Prejudice*. The stuff that filled the books in my library.

It still felt surreal that a chance encounter with Gavin had brought me to this moment. A secret desire, an unrequited crush . . . that was all it was supposed to be.

"You're quiet," Cooper said. "Nervous?"

I shook my head. "Not very. Anymore, at least."

"Then how are you feeling about all this?" He gestured around us.

"Surprisingly good."

I wondered if Gavin had filled him in on my initial refusal. I was guessing so. It didn't seem like these two men kept things from each other. Watching the way they silently communicated, reading each other through unspoken glances and nods, made me doubt there were many secrets between them. Still, I wanted to be honest with Cooper.

"It's all a little odd, sure, but it's nice. You have a good eye for dresses." I ran my hand over the delicate beading on my thigh.

"Years of practice." He nodded. "But don't worry, I get how you're feeling. It's always strange at first, but you can trust me. If I—or anyone else—ever make you feel uncomfortable, I want you to tell me."

I offered him a soft smile, more than a little appreciative of the reassurance. "This literacy event is important to me. You know my library—"

"Gavin told me," he cut in with a grin. "It's important work you do. We're happy to be contributing."

Another roll of warmth took hold of me and I nodded. "Thanks. So ... anything I should expect tonight?"

He shrugged. "Important as the cause is, it's much like any other fundraiser. You can expect lots of greedy politicians, money-hungry businessmen, and cheap, terrible champagne."

I chuckled. "That's fine. I'm not much of a drinker."

"We'll stay an hour or so. I don't want you to be uncomfortable, so I'll stick by your side the entire time. Mainly it's just an excuse to shake hands, exchange business cards, and let those who run in these circles know about our services."

I nodded. It seemed straightforward enough.

When we arrived, I was grateful the driver dropped us off right in front of the building. I wasn't used to wearing these heels and had a feeling my feet would be crying by the end of the evening.

Inside the ballroom, I was dazzled by the crystal chandelier hanging from the ceiling, the seven-piece band playing smooth jazz on the stage, and all the sophisticated people mingling around us. Though, I had to note, nobody was wearing a gown quite as beautiful as mine.

I might have been out of my element, but I sure didn't look like it. It was only then that it hit me exactly how sweet and thoughtful Cooper's gesture was. Thinking about wearing one of the cocktail dresses hanging in my closet made me wince. I'd have stuck out like a sore thumb.

"Something to drink?" a white-jacketed waiter asked, balancing a tray of champagne flutes beside us.

Cooper appraised me silently, waiting for my response.

"Please." I accepted a glass and brought it to my lips. The chilled bubbles were just what I needed to calm the last of my remaining nerves.

Cooper refused a glass and led me over toward a group of men. He seemed to recognize one of them, because he shook his hand while the guy smiled broadly at him.

"You staying out of trouble?" the man asked. He was around my father's age, with salt-and-pepper hair and a belly that pushed out his tuxedo jacket.

"Just barely. You know me." Cooper grinned.

"Gentlemen, this is a man you need to know. He and his brothers have a harem of beauties at their beck and call. Take his card. Give him a call. Trust me on this one," the man said to the group.

"Speaking of which, this is Emma. Emma, this is Bill Mitchell."

Bill's gazed trailed over me, but just as I started to tense up, I felt the comforting warmth of Cooper's hand on the small of my back and remembered the thousand bucks I had coming to me. I was here with a date and was under no obligation to ever go on another, least of all with this dirty old man. This was just a job like any other, and I was in total control.

The reminder made it a whole lot easier to stretch my lips into a cool smile.

"Pleasure."

Mitchell elbowed the man next to him. "The pleasure is all mine."

Cooper handed a business card to each of the men, murmuring things like *very discreet* and *we guarantee your satisfaction*.

As strange as it should have been, the encounter felt less like a sales pitch and more like a secret handshake in a good-old-boys' club. I brushed it off easily, but maybe that was due to Cooper's inherent charm.

Moments later, he led me across the ballroom toward another group he'd spotted.

"Do you enjoy working with your brothers?" I asked, still thinking of the men's eager faces as they'd grabbed cards from Cooper's waiting fingers. "It's an odd business. To be family-run, I mean."

Cooper smirked that lopsided grin I was coming to like. "I guess it is a little weird. But I like working with them . . . some days. Other times, they drive me fucking nuts. I think that's normal, though. Who likes their siblings one hundred percent of the time?"

"How did you guys get involved in . . . what you do?" I didn't want to sound judgmental, because truly, I was only curious.

His eyes met mine, appraising me, as we joined a group of men in front of the bar. Then Cooper leaned down to whisper, "Hold that thought."

After we had a similar conversation with this group of men, Cooper led me away once again, but this time toward a high-top table overlooking the action, and pulled out a bar stool for me.

"Your feet must be killing you," he said, glancing down at my heels.

I let out a thankful sigh. "How did you know?"

"My mom wore heels to work every night. Sometimes, when she'd get home, she'd ask me to rub her feet if I was still up."

I smiled. "You're a good son."

"I was." He smiled too, sadly. "She's been gone for many years."

"I'm sorry. Do you miss her?" The moment the words left my lips, I wanted to smack myself. What a stupid question. Of course he missed her. But Cooper surprised me, thinking it over for a long moment before answering.

"In some ways."

His response struck me as strange. I'd expected him to say *very much so*, or *every day*. Instead, it sounded like he wasn't quite sure.

"We had an interesting upbringing."

"Interesting, how?" I asked, unsure if I was

overstepping.

"It was *colorful*. But it's not my place to fill you in. If it were just you and me spending time together, it would be one thing. With Gavin in the mix . . . he's more private than I am. He might not appreciate me opening those doors. I'll let him decide how much he wants to share on that front."

I tensed at the mention of his name and forced a smile. "And you think he'll tell me?"

Cooper looked thoughtful for a moment, considering it. "If you win his trust, he will."

As much as Gavin grated on my nerves and shook me up from the inside out, there it was again. The lure of a mystery. It sounded like an interesting challenge.

"Noted," I replied.

Cooper waved to someone across the room, and moments later a familiar-looking man strode toward us. I could almost hear the sound of ovaries exploding in his wake and knew right away that they were related. After all, he had Gavin and Cooper's height and their chiseled good looks. He wasn't as stern as Gavin, nor was he as playful as Cooper. He was somewhere in between.

"Emma, this is Quinn. My oldest brother."

The gorgeous and intimidating Quinn took my hand in his large palm. "Damn. They make me sound ancient. I'm thirty-six, not dead, motherfucker."

When he shot me a smile—complete with straight white teeth, blue eyes, and a dimple—my knees went weak. They were all beautiful. Tall. Handsome. Deadly to the libido.

"It's nice to meet you," I managed.

"You as well," Quinn said, still holding my hand. He reluctantly released me a few seconds later, but I was thankful none of the butterflies that swamped my senses when Gavin was near seemed to erupt.

"Is Gavin here too?" Not that I cared. I just hadn't expected to see him tonight, but since both his brothers were here . . .

"No." Cooper shook his head. "We usually split up these types of appearances. We'd never have a night to ourselves if we had to attend them all."

Quinn nodded. "Divide and conquer. And on that note, if you'll excuse me, I have a few people I need to catch up with. It was nice to meet you, Emma."

"You as well."

"You doing okay so far? Or are you ready to get out of here?" Cooper asked before I had the chance to ponder it more.

"I'm okay. I just feel a little . . . out of place." I looked down at my lap, smoothing my hands over my dress again.

Cooper's gaze darkened. "Do you see those men looking at you, princess?" He nodded toward the corner of the room where a cluster of three men in business suits were watching us—or rather, me.

I nodded, feeling his fingers return to my lower back.

"It's because you're beautiful. You know that?"

I turned toward him, my cheeks flushing. "I forgot to thank you for the dress."

"It has nothing to do with the dress. You could be dressed in a garbage sack and still be the most beautiful woman in the room."

My blush deepened. "Thank you."

For the next while, we made the rounds of the room. He introduced me to people he knew and we chatted casually with groups of men and women, with Cooper handing off his card surreptitiously when the opportunity arrived.

True to his word, though, he led me toward the exit just over an hour later. He had the gift of small talk and was lethally charming, but I was grateful the night didn't drag on. The weight of hungry gazes was heavy, and I was already feeling drained. I was quite surprised, however, that we didn't stay for the five-thousand-dollar-per-plate dinner Gavin had told me about. Then again, Cooper wasn't impressed with the champagne, and I had a feeling he'd be even less so with the food. And the last thing I wanted to do was sit around a table listening to stuffy conversation.

On the way home, he asked if I was hungry. When I said yes, he directed the limo driver to pull into a plaza where there were several chain restaurants and a few fast-food places.

"Burgers or tacos?" he asked.

My stomach growled. "A cheeseburger sounds pretty great, actually."

Cooper instructed our driver again through the intercom, and soon we were pulling away from the drive-through with two cheeseburgers, fries, and bottles of water. We ate together and chatted easily during the ride home.

It was strange how smoothly tonight had gone, in spite of everything—and even more surprising was how well I got along with Cooper. What little I knew of him, he seemed like one of the good guys. Those were hard to find these days.

When the limo pulled to a stop in front of my brownstone, Cooper opened the door and climbed out to escort me up the steps.

I paused on the stoop, unsure what might happen next. "I had a great time."

"I did too." He brought my hand to his lips, pressing a soft kiss there, and for a moment I thought he might pull away and cup my cheek to bring me in for a full, intimate kiss.

I wet my lips, unsure what I was feeling. Curiosity? Desire? Gratitude that he'd made me feel so comfortable?

Leaning toward me, Cooper pressed a soft kiss to my mouth, lingering there but not deepening the kiss, not taking—just asking.

"Good night, princess," he murmured, pulling away reluctantly.

"Night."

Letting myself inside my dark house, I closed and locked the door, then pressed my back against it and heaved out a sigh, my brain in overdrive.

My date with Cooper had gone well, though it had left me with more questions than answers where Gavin was concerned. But what did that matter? It was like I was looking for trouble, and that needed to stop. Things had gone swimmingly. Date one, down, and true to his word, Cooper hadn't tried to sleep with me.

So, why couldn't I shake the feeling that I should end this all here and now? Before my next date? Before this got out of hand?

Maybe I really didn't want an adventure after all. Maybe I still wasn't over everything that had happened with Nathan. Maybe I needed more time.

Hell, who was I kidding? There was only one reason I was all in knots.

And that reason?

Was named Gavin Kingsley.

Chapter Eight

Cooper

Stripping my tie free from my shirt collar after a long day, I let out a tired groan. This week had kicked my ass. Between work, my nonexistent social life, and the punishing kick-boxing workouts I forced myself through, I was ready to relax.

The one bright spot? Emma. She'd turned out to be the perfect companion for the event last weekend, able to keep up with conversations on wide-ranging topics from politics to literature to professional football. It was impressive. As a librarian, she was well-read, and though she was quiet, there was a deep intelligence that burned beneath the surface. I found it incredibly sexy.

We talked, we laughed, we ate . . . hell, even that had been sexy. No daintily eaten salad for Emma. She bit into that cheeseburger like a champ. Even made a cute little groaning sound when she chewed that had the blood rushing from my head straight south.

All in all, it was a great evening. Emma might need the money, but she was both beautiful as well as cultured—far more so than me or my brothers. We were raised on the wrong side of the tracks, but that didn't stop us from trying to infiltrate the upper-crust East Coast scene. And with the right clothes, Emma had fit in perfectly.

I'd come into this idea thinking I'd nudge my brother back into the real world again. Get him excited about Emma and life. But she really might be a great asset for us.

My brain shot back to the end of the night when I'd walked her to her door. I didn't know what had possessed me. Maybe it was the way her tongue had swiped that full bottom lip. Or the delicious scent that had been pouring off her skin all night. Whatever the reason, I couldn't help myself. I'd bent low and brushed my mouth against hers.

It was a bad move. It only made me want more. For her to invite me inside so I could explore those sweet curves . . . find out if I could get her to groan like she had in the car. To see exactly what she looked like under that dress.

But I could read the indecision written all over her face, so I didn't press for more. If Gavin decided he truly didn't want her? Of course I would sleep with her, but only when she was begging me for it. I wasn't about to play second best to anyone.

And who knew? That day might come sooner rather than later. I'd only seen them together for a few minutes one time. Maybe I'd misread things and he really didn't give a shit.

I toweled off quickly and swiped the steam off the mirror to floss, but then my cell phone vibrated from its spot on the granite vanity. I shot a glance at the screen and realized I'd missed some texts and a call, all within the last thirty minutes.

All from Gavin.

I let out a laugh and shook my head. Wasn't there some saying about curiosity killing the cat?

Chapter Nine

Emma

"Get that booty down. Give me ten more!" Tony barked.

I huffed out a breath, straightening the plank position I held until my stomach muscles quivered and my thighs screamed in protest.

Bethany let out a grunt beside me, and I shot her an icy glare. She'd gotten us into this mess, talking me into a buy-one-get-one-free coupon at the new gym near the library. Now we were in personal-training-session number two of ten we'd purchased, and I had no idea how I could make it through eight more of these. I was about three seconds away from running for the bathroom to toss my cookies. It was only the memory of that late-night burger and fries that kept me going.

"Three, two, one. Good job, ladies," Tony said, satisfied.

Exhausted, I collapsed onto the mat in a trembling heap.

"See you on Thursday." Tony sauntered away, clearly proud of himself for the level of torture he'd inflicted on us.

"That wasn't so bad, right?" Bethany grinned, sitting up.

"You might have to carry me out of here, but other than that, yeah, it was great." I rolled my eyes. I couldn't wait to get home, shower, and collapse into bed with an ice pack.

When Tony had asked about our fitness goals, Bethany had spouted something inspiring about wanting to be stronger. My goals weren't so lofty. I just wanted to look better naked, but I figured saying my goal was sex with the lights on wasn't going to cut it.

"I need those updates you promised me," Bethany said, toweling the sweat off her forehead.

I'd successfully dodged her questions all day about my "date" with Cooper this past weekend, feigning that I was too busy to get into it, but now she knew no one was at home waiting for me, and my time was hers.

Turning to face her on the mat, I pulled my knees to

my chest. "It was actually really nice. He was a perfect gentleman, easy to talk to, and we got along well."

"Did he kiss you?" She grinned.

A tiny rush of butterflies hit my belly. "He did. It was . . . nice." I hadn't been kissed softly like that, so tenderly, in what felt like forever.

"What's next?"

"I have an event I'm supposed to attend with Gavin."

"Look at you. Just jumping right in. I love it."

I rolled my eyes. "Don't be like that. You know this is—"

"All for the house," Bethany repeated in a mocking tone. "Right, I'm just saying, getting your toes wet is good. It's going to help you take the big leap into real-life dating."

"I wouldn't hold your breath." I grabbed my own towel, but used it as a pillow to collapse back onto my yoga mat.

"Em, it's almost been a year since—"

"Don't say his name," I blurted. Then, realizing how silly that was—what was he, Voldemort?—I sat up and said, "Look, I'll date eventually, but this isn't dating. It's a business arrangement to fix my grandmother's brownstone and bring it back to its former glory. Seriously, who in their right mind would agree to be a tether ball between two intimidatingly hot and oversexed brothers?"

Who, indeed?

Despite my words, I was only half convinced that my own reasons were quite as pure as I was making them out to be. What if I was just a glutton for punishment?

I flopped my arm over my eyes as Bethany let out a squeal.

"So, they're oversexed? And intimidatingly hot, huh? I knew it." She raised her eyebrows.

I let out an agitated sigh. "I can't say anything around you, can I?"

"Fine, fine, I'll let up, but tell me this. Are you nervous?"

I considered her question. When I logged in to my

bank account this morning and saw the thousand-dollar deposit from FD Industries, I'd felt strange, but not strange enough to call the whole thing off.

Money like that was going to restore all the moldings in my house and maybe even get a few of the rooms a new coat of paint. And that was just from one night. If I could get through ten dates, the place could really be the home I wanted it to be—the safe, warm space I remembered.

And after Nathan? I needed someplace safe and warm.

Even more of a reason to stay the hell away from Gavin Kingsley, a little voice in my head whispered.

I shut that voice down and focused back on Bethany, moving my arm from my eyes to consider her question.

Was I nervous?

"Not exactly."

"Anxious, then," Bethany countered.

"Nope."

But as I thought of Gavin's brooding sexuality, his

intense stares and cool demeanor, a rush of goose bumps broke out over my skin. He wasn't warm, wasn't like the sweet, smiling Cooper, and there was no hope of a fast-food date afterward. Worse? I wasn't sure I wanted there to be. Part of me was growing addicted to the seasick feeling inside me when I thought of him. Like an ache so deep, there was only one way to make it stop.

I swallowed hard and shook my head. "Why should I be?"

Bethany's brows pulled together. "Because they're like . . . sharing you?"

A hot shiver raced over my skin that had absolutely nothing to do with my workout. "Like I said, I'm a hired companion. I'm not *dating* them both."

She nodded, still looking unsure. "And they're both okay with this?"

Bethany knew the entire arrangement. My first instinct had been to guard their proposal like a secret, but I knew I needed advice and someone to turn to in case things got messy. Bethany was that person for me. It's not like I could tell my mother about Forbidden Desires and the men who ran it.

I chewed on my lip. "Yeah. It's not sexual or romantic. I'm just like a walking billboard. That's all. I have to smile and be pretty, and then they fork over the cash to fix my place. Simple."

She stretched her arms over her head. "Right . . . but if real feelings start to develop, I doubt this arrangement will continue to work. Someone will be left odd man out, and if these guys are even half as alpha—or how did you put it—oversexed and intimidating—"

I shoved her in the side, but she pressed on, laughing.

"—as I think they are, that won't work. No one likes to be runner-up."

That wouldn't happen. So what if Cooper had given me a little peck on the mouth? That hardly meant they were competing for me.

Bethany went on, heedless of my silence. "What's this event you're attending with Gavin, anyway?"

"I really don't know much. It's a charity thing. Honestly, I'm not sure what to wear. This is all so out of my element."

"What did you wear to the first one?"

We rose to our feet, heading to the locker room to retrieve our car keys and cell phones.

"Cooper sent me a gown."

"Nice. No gown from Gavin?" she asked, one brow arched.

"No." Gavin didn't strike me as a send-a-gown type of guy, and somehow it didn't seem okay to wear the same gown Cooper had given me on a date with Gavin. I'd probably head to the department store and see if I could find anything suitable on the clearance rack.

"From what you told me, it seems that Cooper is the sweet, thoughtful one. So, why do I get the feeling that you're more drawn to the alpha-hole?"

"The alpha-hole?" I asked, fishing a dollar bill out of my wallet so I could pay for a water on the way out.

"Alpha asshole." Bethany shot me a knowing wink. "But don't dodge the question. Which of them do you like better?"

Avoiding her eyes, I handed a dollar to the front-desk attendant and accepted a water bottle in return, but my brain was elsewhere. A wave of icy nerves prickled my skin. Once we were outside, I shielded my eyes from the sun and met Bethany's gaze.

"They're all so different, to be honest," I said, hedging as best I could. How was I supposed to reply to a question I didn't even know the answer to?

"All," she asked, her eyes widening. "How many are there?"

I laughed. "Three. And all three Kingsley brothers are drop-dead gorgeous. I met their older brother, Quinn, at the event too."

"Can I have the spare?" she asked, chuckling. "Unless, of course, you're going to date him too."

"Stop it!" I said, my cheeks glowing with heat. "I'm totally not. And it's going to be fine. I told you, we're going on dates, but none of us are dating."

"Hmm." Bethany nodded, contemplating. There was something in her hesitation that nagged at me.

"What?" I asked.

"I'll just be interested to see where this all goes, that's all. I want you to be careful. After Nathan and all—"

I cut in with a nod. "I will be."

And with that ominous warning ringing in my head, we said our good-byes and I headed for the bus stop. All the way home, Bethany's urging to be careful played through my brain.

Cooper had been sweet and thoughtful, sending me a beautiful gown to wear accompanied with a handwritten note. So, why was my mind squarely focused on Gavin? There was something about his steely demeanor that called to me. It was like being given a locked box and being told not to open it. You'd quickly become obsessed with getting inside it.

Which of them did I like better?

There was no doubt my date with Cooper had been everything a date should be. He was easy—charming and fun. But more than all of that? He was thoughtful. I liked that. Liked it more than I was willing to admit.

But that didn't change the fact that I'd been lusting after Gavin for almost a year. And it had been a year spent wondering if he was smart, strong, and confident—only to discover he was so much more.

He was dominant and gruff and mysterious. Everything Cooper wasn't. If it weren't for their stunning good looks, I might never have known they were brothers.

Not that any of it mattered. I didn't have to like either of them, and I certainly wasn't getting involved with either.

In fact, I was going to stop thinking about them both.

Starting now.

Chapter Ten

Gavin

"Fucking Cooper," I muttered under my breath.

Dragging the towel off my hips, I swiped away the steam covering my bathroom mirror. The reflection staring back at me was laced with frustration.

I blew out a pissed-off breath and fought to erase my scowl. Sonja was always saying it was going to age me early. She joked that I'd need Botox if I kept that up. I assured her I didn't give a shit about that, yet her nagging had apparently gotten through. I relaxed my features and took another deep breath.

I wanted to pretend the reason I was pissed was because I'd let Cooper talk me into this. But I knew it was a little more complicated than that. *Fuck*. Okay, a lot more complicated.

After stepping into a pair of black Armani boxer briefs, I shrugged into a crisp white dress shirt and left it unbuttoned as I strode into the formal dining room and straight toward the liquor cabinet. This room was rarely ever used, I think I'd only eaten at the table once, but the large oak cabinet opposite the dining table held all my favorite bottles of liquor.

Selecting a cut-crystal glass, I let out another sigh and rolled my shoulders.

I'd tried to shake the feeling, to convince myself that it was all in my head, but something about tonight felt too much like the way things had started three years ago. With Ashley. I hadn't been truly involved with an escort since we'd been together. Not that I allowed myself to think of her often.

Something about Emma stirred up those same feelings inside me, and this situation was eerily similar. Of course, I would never have let Cooper touch Ashley. She was mine. Which was exactly why Emma couldn't be. I couldn't go down that road again.

So then, why did you blow up his phone the other night trying to find out about their date?

Fucking idiot. It wasn't like I could ask him if they'd fucked. It was none of my business, but part of me hoped that when I heard his voice or he responded that I'd be able to tell. There would be some mocking note there, or a swagger.

The point was moot, though, because the prick never called me back that night, and didn't say a word about her all week. Which was fine.

Again, none of my concern.

And remembering Ashley now only drove that point home.

As I poured myself a measure of bourbon, my brain cataloged the similarities between her and Emma. Sky-blue eyes that were so bright, they were striking. Long, shiny dark hair. A feisty but decidedly submissive nature—it was that last part that got my blood roaring south.

The way things ended with Ashley were messy, and I couldn't go through that again. Yes, there were many things I loved about her, her fondness for rough sex not the least among them. Her fondness for prescription drugs, though? That had been a deal breaker.

She'd been a ballerina who'd aged out of the system, as gorgeous and graceful as anyone might expect with cheekbones that could cut glass. She and her fellow dancers had never been shy about partying and smoking, but when all her friends went back on tour and she was left alone? That was when the trouble began.

It was my fault from the start. I knew better. The girls were for fun and fun alone. But deep down, in my own way, I knew I had loved her, even if I'd never told her. In the end, I couldn't save her, and even now, years later, that wound still burned white hot whenever my thoughts turned to her.

Taking a long swallow of bourbon, I appreciated the bitter sting on my tongue, needed it to ground myself.

Emma wasn't Ashley.

And even if I did want to cross that line with Emma? To possess her and make her mine?

I'd promised my brother I wouldn't.

Picking up my phone, I dialed my driver. "I'll be ready in ten. See you out front."

"Yes, Mr. Kingsley," he said before disconnecting the call.

Drink in hand, I headed to the master closet to continue getting ready. Selecting a black tuxedo and a ruby-colored tie, I finished dressing for the event, then tossed back the remainder of my drink in a single gulp. After adding platinum cuff links and my watch, I flipped off the lights and headed out to meet Ben, my driver.

The ride to her brownstone was a short and silent one. I scrolled through my emails, checking for anything new, but there was nothing.

I typed out a text to Cooper.

Can't believe you talked me into this.

His reply came almost instantly.

Have fun, Cooper wrote. *You remember what that is, right?*

Vaguely, I replied.

She's easy. You'll have a good time.

What the fuck does that mean? I typed before deleting it with a snarl. It was none of my business and exactly what he wanted. To yank my chain.

How easy? I finally typed.

I waited, feeling like a caged bear as three little dots

danced across my screen. Finally, his response popped up.

I wouldn't know. Maybe you'll find out and can tell me . . .

His reply contained a winking face that made me want to punch the motherfucker square in the jaw. I hadn't done that in years, not in at least a decade. Back then, our most bitter arguments were settled with our fists. Now we settled our differences like men, punishing each other with stony silence or degrading jabs exchanged over cocktails.

I rolled my eyes. If he was trying to goad me into breaking our deal, it wasn't going to work. I knew the rules, and so did he.

But the realization that he hadn't touched her . . . *Shit.* Why did that excite me so much? The idea of being the first of us to touch her, to hear her cry out in pleasure—in pain? I pulled a deep breath into my lungs. The limo rolled to a stop, and I shoved my phone inside my jacket pocket.

It was go time.

Ben opened the car door, and I climbed out just in time to watch a graceful Miss Emma Bell navigate the row of steps down from her ancient little brownstone. She was a woman who could appreciate fine details. I liked that about her already, although we'd barely exchanged six sentences despite our nearly year-long non-affair.

I leaned against the black limo, sizing Emma up. She was in a wine-colored dress that fell to the ground and was tied in a bow behind her neck. It was simple. Elegant. Perfect.

The curves of her hourglass figure made my palms itch. The desire to reach out and touch her, to see if her creamy skin was as soft as it looked, was a sharp pulse of need. One that I quickly tamped down. That would have to wait. We were headed out to support one of my favorite charities, not to slap our private parts together until we both came in a hot, sticky mess.

Damn. Being an adult was a motherfucker sometimes.

I forced out my most respectable tone. "Good evening, Miss Bell. You're looking well."

She paused before me, dipping her chin so her eyes were trained on my shoes, her perfect submission frustratingly intriguing.

"You are as well, Mr. Kingsley."

Finally, that blazing blue gaze came to rest on mine. I couldn't help but wonder what she saw when she looked at me. Couldn't help but wonder what she thought about during all those coffee-shop run-ins.

"Gavin is fine," I said, correcting her, and she nodded. "Shall we go?"

I took her hand, helping her into the waiting limo before sliding in behind her. Once inside, Emma scooted to the far side, leaving a healthy space between us as Ben pulled out into traffic.

"We match," she murmured.

"Hmm?"

"Your tie." She gestured toward me.

I nodded. She was observant. "Tell me something interesting about you, Emma. Other than the fact you like tea."

She smirked like she knew something I didn't. "Books are my passion."

"Reading them? Smelling them?" I offered her a

small grin. "I've heard that's a thing."

She returned my smile easily, her eyes crinkling in the corners. In that moment, she looked so young, so vulnerable, that for a second I almost called this whole thing off. *Almost.*

"All of the above. Someday I'd like to write one too. I have about a dozen half-finished manuscripts sitting on my hard drive that'll never see the light of day."

"What do you write about?"

"Love," she said, then apparently realizing that she'd exposed more of herself than she meant to, her posture straightened.

"See, that's where we differ," I said.

"You don't believe in love?" she asked, her tone skeptical.

"I do, actually. I just believe it to be rare."

"I agree with you. It's a rare gem to be savored once you've finally found it. I believe that you could spend your entire life looking for it, and never come across it. I find that to be heartbreaking. But if you finally find it, maybe the rarity ... doesn't that make it all the better?" She raised her eyebrows.

"And that inspires your writing?" I asked.

"Yes," she said resolutely. Then she looked down at her delicate hands, the silence growing between us. "I probably sound so stupid, given what you do for a living. It's not about love at all for you, is it?"

I cleared my throat before responding. I appreciated the level of candor between us, how comfortable she was prodding me. I'd been on many dates with many escorts over the years, and ninety-nine percent of them sat silently on the ride to the event, quietly looking at their phones. In that tiny scrap of a clutch, I wasn't even confident Emma had brought her phone along.

"Have you ever heard the saying 'don't judge a book by its cover'?"

"Touché."

I was still kicking myself for revealing that much of myself. Why even tell her I was familiar with love? That wasn't what we were embarking on, and confusing the issue could only complicate things. This book and this cover were a perfect match nowadays, and that was all she needed to know.

I made a mental note to avoid such discussion in the future.

As the limo slowed to a stop, I couldn't help but notice the small smile playing on her lips. "We're here. Are you ready to mingle?"

She nodded. "Let's do this."

On the sidewalk in front of the banquet hall, I offered my arm to her, and after she placed her hand on my forearm, we made our way inside.

The room was a wall of bodies, which was good. It meant a lot of donations were going to come in tonight. But it was also bad because it meant we'd be jockeying for position all night as I tried to make my way through the crowd.

Emma's eyes widened at the scene before us. The line for the bar was at least thirty people deep, and there was barely enough room for us to stand without bumping into someone. They needed a bigger venue next year. It was a good problem to have, though a little bit annoying for this year's guests.

"Would you like something to drink?"

Her gaze went to the long wait at the bar. "I'm not much of a drinker."

"Something mild, then? Unless you want tea?" I was rambling, and I never fucking rambled. When she shot me a look, I placed my hand on the small of her back. "I have an idea."

I signaled an approaching waiter who was delivering cheap champagne on a metal tray, and slipped him a fifty-dollar bill. "Go behind the bar. Make the lady a Shirley Temple with grenadine and a splash of champagne. The good stuff, not this shit you're serving out here. And I'll take a glass of the best bourbon you have. No ice."

Emma glanced at me from the corner of her eye, but didn't say a thing.

"That okay with you?" I asked as the waiter darted away like my money was burning a hole in his pocket.

"It's perfect. Very sweet of you."

"That's a new one for me." I laughed.

"No one's ever called you sweet?"

I thought long and hard about it. "Honestly, no."

"Maybe I bring out a new side of you."

She was being cheeky, and I added it to the growing list of things I liked about her.

"Maybe you do," I agreed.

As we made our way slowly through the crowd toward the front of the ballroom and the stage, Emma's hand came to rest automatically on my arm again. Another item on the list of things I liked.

My extra donation had nsured we'd have seats for tonight's live auction. The event was standing-room only, aside from a few rows of white folding chairs in front of the stage. It was where the serious bidders sat.

Before we could make it up front, our waiter returned in record time with our cocktails.

I tipped him again. "Bring us another round in fifteen minutes."

He nodded, darting away again.

I watched while Emma took a sip from her champagne flute, tasting her drink.

"Well?"

She broke into a grin. "So yummy. I think this is my new favorite drink."

I didn't have the heart to tell her that it was basically a kiddo cocktail with a splash of champagne. I wasn't sure if she'd heard me order it. Then again, there was something I liked about the fact that she wasn't a drinker. After some of the shit I'd dealt with, it was a weight off my shoulders.

I glanced at her smiling face as she surveyed the room, then noticed the pool of men who'd already noticed her. They looked at her like she was the biggest, juiciest steak they'd ever seen, and I placed an arm around her protectively, as if to show them she wasn't for sale.

Not this one.

Except ... wasn't she? She'd essentially been blackmailed into coming here, and it was all my fault. Frowning down at her, I paused.

"Do you really want to be here right now? I know I

can be overbearing sometimes, and if this arrangement doesn't work for you . . ."

Her gaze searched mine. "I really want to be here." Her tone was sincere.

"Okay. We don't have to stay long. Let's find our seats for the auction."

As we weaved our way through the crowd, hand in hand, I realized there was already something that felt very different about this. I already knew I was intrigued with Emma, but now I knew that she was someone of substance, it seemed to matter even more what she thought of me. That was a first. I normally never gave a shit what someone thought of me, but with her? Somehow that mattered.

"Kingsley!" a man's voice behind us boomed.

We turned, and I met the gaze of a man in his late fifties with a short graying beard.

"Mr. Thornton. Good evening." I turned and squeezed Emma's hand. "Do you want to find our seats? We're 6A and B. I'll see you in just a moment."

She nodded and turned to saunter off.

Thornton was a top-notch client. A huge moneymaker for our business.

So then, why couldn't I tear my gaze away from the sway of little Emma Bell's luscious hips?

Chapter Eleven

Emma

I'd fantasized about Gavin constantly for almost a year, but now that I had his attention, everything had changed. Sipping my drink, I let my gaze wander around the room. Gavin had directed me here to a chair near the stage and made sure I was okay, saying that there was someone he needed to talk to.

As I sat waiting for the auction to begin, I enjoyed my sweet, fizzy drink and the atmosphere around me, marveling yet again at how different everything was from my everyday life.

Any moment, I expected the clock to strike twelve and everything around me would dissolve, the limo turning back into a pumpkin, my dress turning back into my boring black-and-white work clothes. But that wasn't going to happen.

Tonight, I was freshly waxed, manicured, and wearing a fine gown. I'd had two nights like this in as many weeks with two sexy men.

Was this real life?

It certainly didn't feel like it.

Holding tightly to the stem of my champagne glass, I glanced back toward the crowd of people, hoping to spot Gavin. It took less than a second until I found him, still talking with the man from before.

When we locked eyes from across the room, a shiver of raw heat pulsed through me. It reminded me so much of the way he'd looked when he dropped that card into the jar at the coffee shop, like there was an intimate secret between us.

His eyes darkened with unmistakable heat, and his long fingers reached down to adjust a cuff link on his wrist while he continued to watch me. A hot shiver raced through me in anticipation. He exuded power and strength, and I was weak, unable to resist him.

The way he looked at me—predatory and hungry—was like no man ever had. It wasn't in that way other men might, leering and curious. There was no curiosity. Gavin knew. If he wanted me, he would have me, and I would be powerless to stop him.

I was a doe and he was a lion, stalking toward me with determined strides that made my knees go weak, even as I sat in my chair.

Heat spread from my face to my core, and for a moment I was worried Gavin could read me like a book. But then he smiled and another wave of traitorous desire rolled through me, making butterflies swirl in my stomach. I softened.

Dear God, I like his smile. I wanted to make him do that again.

"Everything okay?" he asked, sliding into the seat beside me.

"Yes, fine."

I took the final sip of my drink just as the waiter delivered our next round, and Gavin gave me an approving nod as I traded glasses.

Again, he slipped a tip onto the waiter's tray, and I watched as the guy scurried away, ready to jump at

Gavin's beck and call. Just like everyone else seemed to.

That was when it hit me. Gavin was a *man*.

I'd dated *guys* before. Their needs always came first, and I was merely an afterthought. I knew things with Gavin would be different. Maybe it was because his job was managing relationships with women, making sure they were safe and taken care of, but I wasn't sure. Whatever the reason, all my senses were humming. This man had my complete attention.

"How was your evening with Cooper?" Gavin's full mouth quirked up just a fraction. It didn't escape my notice that he didn't refer to it as a date.

"It was nice. We had fun."

He raised an eyebrow.

"He took me to the drive-through on the way home." I shrugged. "We shared french fries."

Gavin smirked and shook his head. "He really knows how to woo a woman."

"I don't think he was trying to woo me."

"Don't you?"

Gavin's expression turned serious, and for a moment, I didn't understand the game we were playing.

"What did you talk about?" he asked.

Why were we even talking about this? Was he trying to set me up with his brother? If he wanted me to fall for Cooper, then why agree to go out with me himself?

I shrugged again. "He mentioned something about your *colorful* upbringing."

Gavin cleared his throat. "Did he now?"

I nodded. "He made it sound so fascinating. Not at all like the piano lessons and strict curfew I grew up with. Though, to be honest, I can't picture you all growing up with hippie-type parents or something." I grinned, imagining the Kingsley brothers younger and in some sort of drum circle.

He let out a choked laugh and shifted in his seat. "Yeah, no. It was nothing like that. To be honest, things were pretty desolate those first few years."

Cooper hadn't made it sound that way. Though, he had mentioned something about earning Gavin's trust . . . God, I felt stupid now. I wanted to shove my words back in my mouth and pretend I'd never said them, but Gavin was glancing at the stage, speaking as casually as ever.

"We were raised by a single mom, and times were tough. Not such an unusual story. But it made us determined to make something of ourselves."

Gavin rising out of poverty sounded so dashing. This was probably just his way of steering us away from a too-personal topic. But deep down, as much as I didn't want to care about him or his childhood, part of me knew what he said was true, and my heart gave a squeeze.

I took a gulp of my drink. There was a reason they called it liquid courage.

Gavin's hot gaze fell on me, appraising my reaction to his revelation. "If you haven't figured it out yet, we grew up on the wrong side of the tracks. I'm sure my childhood was a far cry from the country-club lunches and tennis lessons you enjoyed."

I blinked. *Ouch.* I'd clearly overstepped. "I'm sorry."

"Don't be," he said, but before I got the chance to explain myself, the lights on the stage went up and, just like that, the auction began, leaving a heavy silence hanging between us.

The hostess began with an overview of the charity we were here to support. I suddenly felt foolish that I hadn't researched the reason we were here. As I listened to the woman speak about the topic that was clearly so dear to her heart, my throat felt tight. It was an international charity that helped rescue women from prostitution and human trafficking. From the corner of my eye, I glanced at Gavin, trying to get a read on how he felt about being here, but apparently, this was a speech he'd heard many times before.

A round of polite applause followed a few heart-rending stories about the work the charity had done, and as the auctioneer was introduced, I was tempted to lean over and ask Gavin about why in the hell Forbidden Desires would think this was their kind of crowd.

I knew, of course, that their business wasn't a prostitution racket—it had been discussed with me by more than one person in the past two weeks I'd worked with them. Still, it felt like that sort of distinction might be lost on the crowd at a gala like this.

I shoved aside my apprehension and gave the

important cause the attention it deserved.

The items up for bid were introduced one by one. We watched intently as each was auctioned off to the highest bidder. Fifteen minutes passed, and Gavin hadn't said a word. I wondered if perhaps he would just be a silent spectator, opting not to bid. Heaven knew the items were way out of my income bracket, as much as I might have been inspired to help.

"The final item up for bid tonight is the luxurious seven-night vacation on a private yacht off the coast of the Seychelles islands," the auctioneer said.

Clearly, they had saved the best for last. The large flat screen on the stage showed a massive gleaming-white vessel in turquoise waters so clear and blue, it almost didn't look real.

I'd never heard of the locale before, but the map on the screen showed it was a group of islands in the Indian Ocean off the coast of Africa, and the auctioneer filled in the remaining details—that it was a playground for the rich and famous, and a favorite vacation spot for Britain's royal family.

"We'll start the bidding at twenty thousand dollars."

Gavin surprised me by raising his hand, placing the opening bid.

From there, the bidding went by at a dizzying pace. Apparently, Gavin wasn't the only high roller waiting for the best item tonight.

When the bidding surpassed fifty thousand, my head swam. That was more than I made in a year.

When Gavin raised his hand to the auctioneer's request for a fifty-five-thousand-dollar bid, a wave of nausea rolled through me. The bid went unchallenged, and I watched in amazement as the auctioneer counted down and finally pronounced Gavin the winner.

"We got it." He beamed at me, and I did my best to tamp down my shock and match his enthusiasm.

We? I wasn't going on his worldwide yachting adventure, but good for him. I was glad he was pleased, but I couldn't deny that my head was spinning. This was all so far out of my league, I felt like I'd stepped into a dream.

"There are a few people I need to talk to. That okay

with you?" I vaguely heard him ask.

I nodded. "Of course. That's the reason we're here. But . . ."

"But what?"

The people around us were filing from the seats but Gavin and I stayed put, his hazel gaze locked on mine.

"I was just wondering. Do you really think this is a good outlet for marketing a business like yours? It's none of my business, but—"

"What's that supposed to mean?"

"The people here, aren't they here because they want to end prostitution?"

Gavin frowned. "I can understand your point." Depositing our empty glasses on the tray of a passing waiter, he cleared his throat and added, "But you'd be surprised."

I blinked. "What do you mean?"

"What people fund and what they do . . . they're not always the same. But, to be perfectly candid, I don't really come here for the marketing. It's secondary."

"Then why come?"

He considered my question for a long moment. "This work is important to me. I know that the women we employ are strong and confident professionals, but that doesn't mean that a few don't slip through the cracks. It's . . . personal. A sort of due diligence."

And then it hit me. Given what Gavin did for a living, it was even more important that he become involved with causes like this. His heart was bigger than he made it seem, and I found I respected him even more.

Damn it, do not get soft, Emma. You know what happens when you get soft.

My shoulders tensed and I looked at him. "I never thought about it that way."

"You would have no reason to. Come on, I have to say a few hellos before everyone has gone."

Still reeling from his surprisingly personal revelation, I followed him as we stood and headed back to the ballroom.

Maybe this was another difference between Gavin and Cooper. Cooper had been all about the business, eager to talk to anyone and everyone about what he did. As we made our way toward the crowds of people, though, Gavin's lazy pace made it all too clear he wasn't here for that. Not really.

For him, this was a charity event first and a business event second. It was strangely . . . endearing.

What other surprises did this man have in store for me?

We approached a group of older men and spoke with a few corporate bigwigs. Gavin was smooth and in command, mesmerizing to watch. He didn't have the easy charm Cooper did, but his confidence more than made up for that fact.

"Gavin." A younger man with a crooked smile reached for Gavin's hand. "It's good to see you again."

"You, as well, Mister . . . ?"

The man chuckled. "It's Dave."

"Right. It's good to see you. Let me know if I can help with anything." Almost imperceptibly, he handed the man a card and then ushered me to a new crowd of people.

After several similar brief conversations, we came to yet another group of men old enough to be my father.

"Dr. Barton," Gavin said, extending a hand. "I trust you've been well."

"Not as well as you've been, I see," the older man said, eyeing me eagerly. He had a short goatee and glasses, but his silver hair was the only thing distinguished about him. He leered at me, sizing me up. His gaze roving over my skin made me want to crawl out of it and hang it elsewhere like a suit. Anything to get him to stop staring.

"Not still rooting for the Bruins, are you?" Gavin asked Dr. Barton.

"Of course." The man laughed.

"That's a damn shame," Gavin joked.

They continued teasing each other for several minutes while I stood beside Gavin, smiling politely and trying to blend into the background. But I couldn't escape the unfamiliar and somewhat creepy feeling. Even as he spoke to Gavin, the man's gaze hardly left me . . . or my cleavage.

"If you'll excuse us, we can't stay, but if you're in

need of a companion to an upcoming event, I can help." Gavin handed out his business card again, this time a little more obviously.

Relieved that we were finally close to leaving, I pasted on a polite smile. This process wasn't yet familiar or comfortable, but I was trying. I wasn't sure if this would ever feel natural for me, and in a way, I hoped not.

"And how about a night with her?" Dr. Barton grinned at me through crooked teeth. "What do you say, sweetie?"

Cringing, I stammered. "I—um . . ."

Gavin's arm wrapped around me possessively, gripping my waist to draw me close to the warmth of his body. "She's not available."

Seconds later, he dragged me away, hot anger rolling off him in waves.

Once we were in sight of the front doors, he paused, turning me to face him. His nostrils flaring, he took a deep breath, obviously fighting to get himself under control. But when he spoke, his words surprised me.

"I'm sorry. I have no idea why I acted like that. I had

no right to decide for you. If that's what you want . . ."

It took me a moment to understand what he was saying.

"God, no. I have no interest in that. You saved me. I should be thanking you."

His sharp exhale was confirmation that I'd said the right thing. We were on the same page.

"I'm sure you and Cooper will keep me plenty busy. I'm not interested in anything more than that."

"Good. Ready to get out of here?"

I nodded, but as Gavin watched me, his expression changed from one filled with longing to one laced with . . . *regret*?

I wondered just exactly what it was I was agreeing to. Looking down at my shoes, I fought to compose myself. Tonight had been filled with so many conflicting emotions, I was almost dizzy.

In that moment, I knew this wouldn't be casual, knew I wouldn't walk away from this in one piece.

Using two firm fingers beneath my chin, Gavin

tipped my face up toward him. "Do I frighten you?" he asked, amused.

"Of course not," I lied.

And he didn't.

He terrified me.

I knew, even without truly knowing, that Gavin had the power to hurt me deeply. I could already feel my emotions spinning out of control. Nothing about this situation was normal. But then again, nothing about this man was normal either, so what did I expect?

"Good, because you terrify me," he murmured, taking my hand and pulling me toward the exit.

My breath caught in the back of my throat at his admission, but I was powerless to do anything but follow him to the exit and wonder what tonight had in store for me next.

Chapter Twelve

Emma

The darkened interior of the limo created a quiet, contemplative mood. The moon was high and full, illuminating the leather seats and dim lights of the vehicle, and the farther we got outside of the city, the more brightly the stars shone up above.

Gavin had asked the driver to take us someplace I'd never heard of before. Although I knew I ought to protest—to claim I was tired and wanted to go home—I couldn't bring myself to leave him.

Not yet.

Along the way, I attempted small talk. "I'm sorry if I pried earlier, about your upbringing."

"You're curious." Gavin's voice was smooth, measured.

I nodded. "I wasn't sure what Cooper meant. I asked how it was you came to be involved in this business. I had a feeling there was a story there."

His eyebrows ticked up, but he didn't meet my gaze.

"You're very intuitive."

"Must be the librarian in me. I love a good story."

"Which do you prefer . . . tragedy or romance?"

My smile faded. "I'm not sure I understand what you mean."

He nodded. "In my experience, there's usually not a difference."

Before I could ponder his ominous remark, Gavin took a deep breath and continued.

"First, my upbringing. We were raised by our mother." He paused, his mouth pressed into a firm line. "Never knew who my father was."

"Oh, I'm . . ." The word *sorry* died on my lips.

"Let me guess. You grew up in Connecticut, or upstate New York."

"Upstate."

His lips twisted into a cruel smile. "Here for us. Boston. In an area known for rough neighborhoods and even rougher streets."

Licking my lips, I waited, unsure if I should have started this entire conversation to begin with. It was taking on a darker and more ominous tone than I was prepared for.

I thought that would be the end of our conversation, but Gavin leaned in toward me.

"We deal in the one thing we know—women."

And sex.

He left those words unspoken, but I felt the weight of them press against me as surely as if he'd spoken them aloud. A chill raced down my spine as I was left to wonder what in the hell that meant.

The limo slowed to a stop, parking at the edge of a bluff that looked out over a spread of massive trees below. The twinkling lights of the city glowed faintly in the distance.

"It's beautiful here," I said, more for my own benefit than his. I wanted—no, needed—to change the subject. Needed to see that dark, twisted look in his eyes fade back into the hard determination I'd learned to accept. The look that made me feel less like molten lava inside.

Gavin pressed a button, relieving me of my seat belt, and did the same for his. "Something to drink? Or have you reached your limit?"

The challenge in his words was unmistakable, but that was good. Some indication that he'd come back from wherever it was he'd gone a few moments ago. We both knew I'd had little more than a couple of splashes of champagne, so I grinned at him.

"I think I can handle a little more."

"Perfect." His deep voice was smooth, more hypnotizing than it should have been. Just being here with him felt so surreal.

Gavin opened the wide leather console between us, exposing a hidden refrigerated compartment. He poured a glass of champagne in a long-stemmed flute for me, and a measure of bourbon for himself.

Tapping a few buttons on his phone, Gavin connected his playlist to the limo's sound system. Soft, moody music filled the silence between us.

He was such an intense man, but this moment was so simple—two people sitting in a parked car, listening to music, the moon roof open so we could gaze at the stars. I wanted to ask him what he thought about when he was quiet like this, but I got the sense I'd grilled him enough for one evening. From what I could tell, Gavin wasn't used to opening up about his feelings.

Grasping for a lighter topic, I attempted small talk. "You know my passion, but you never shared your hobbies. What interests you? Other than giving copious amounts of money to charity."

He shifted in his seat to set his glass in the cupholder on the door, and turned toward me. "I'm much more interested in learning about you, to be honest, Miss Bell."

"There's really not much to tell."

"Let's start with why you really agreed to this. What are you looking for?"

"I . . ." I chewed on my bottom lip, trying to think of how best to explain myself. "Okay, this is going to sound a little silly." And only half true, because the rest of my reasoning was buried so deep, even I didn't want to admit it. "The brownstone where you picked me up tonight? I bought it, and it's pretty much falling apart inside."

"And you want to restore it?"

I nodded. "It's more than that, though. The place used to belong to my grandparents. It's been in my family for generations, and my parents were going to just give it up. I could only barely afford it, but I spent so many summers there as a girl ... it felt too important to let someone else make it into some modern, open-concept nightmare of a house."

He considered me for a moment. "That's a good start."

"What do you mean, a good start?"

"That's part of it, I'm sure, but that's not why you're doing this. Not really."

I frowned. "But it is." I looked down, not sure if I knew how to answer his question, unsure that I even wanted to try, but frustrated at how easily he could read me.

Gavin took the champagne glass from my hand and placed it in the cupholder beside his. The air between us changed, the mood becoming something more sinful and insistent.

"Do you want to know what I think?" His voice was low, the rich tone hypnotizing.

I opened my suddenly dry mouth to say no. I didn't want to know what he thought in the least, because some part of me knew he was going to give voice to the very thing I wanted to stay hidden. But being Gavin, he didn't give me a chance to cut in.

"I think you want to feel desired and experience passion, but you're afraid to ask for it. You want a man to take control, to make you feel wanted, and you want to feel pleasure like you've never imagined."

His words stripped me bare, the truth in them startling me to my core. He had me pegged, and it was so cliché, I felt a rush of embarrassment. The lonely little librarian, desperate to experience the kind of passion she'd only read about.

Leaning in closer, Gavin tipped my chin up, drawing my mouth closer to his. I could feel the heat of his skin, his breath ghosting over my lips, and hazy arousal flooded my brain. Cupping my jaw, he brought my lips to his, pressing a soft kiss there—softer than I would have thought possible from him.

When I parted my lips in a silent invitation, Gavin took full control of the kiss, his hot tongue skillfully gliding against mine. We kissed for several moments before he pulled back just an inch, leaving me breathless.

He hummed against the side of my neck as his fingers roamed my skin, light touches meant to pique my interest. And they were doing a damn fine job. "You feel good."

Funny, considering I wasn't doing anything other than sit here, pressed against him, practically panting while he bathed me in gentle caresses.

His hands felt so good on my skin, and it had been so long since I'd been touched like this. Need pulsed between my legs, heavy and hot. I didn't know what was happening to me, only that I'd never felt like this.

"The way you look in that dress?" He made a low sound of approval in his throat. "Those men wanted you. You made me crazy tonight."

"*I* made *you* crazy?" Had he lost it? He was the one so hot, it should be illegal.

"Insane," he murmured, taking my mouth again.

He slanted his jaw, deepening our kiss, his tongue stroking mine until I was dizzy. I'd never been kissed like this. In my less-than-substantial experience, there was always a certain level of fumbling awkwardness when two people first came together. A learning of each other's styles, a give and take.

But there was no awkwardness here. Gavin made himself clear from the first second his mouth met mine. He took. This was a far cry from an exploratory first kiss. He had total control, pulling me close. His hand moved from my jaw to my shoulder, his other stroking the column of my throat.

He smelled of peppermint and leather, and tasted faintly of whiskey. It was an intoxicating combination, and like a lightning flash through the darkness, I was undone.

The rough pads of his fingers slid beneath the satiny material of my halter top, flirting with the ties there, making me crave more of his touch. More contact. More everything.

His mouth was firm and demanding against mine, and I felt the fiery sparks of need detonate deep inside me.

"Damn you for being so fucking tempting."

His whispered dirty words almost undid me. His voice was deep, raw with need, and vibrated through me, making fire lick through every square inch of me, burning me to the core.

Gripping his firm biceps through his jacket, I leaned in for another kiss. He bit my lower lip so hard, I knew it would be bruised tomorrow.

Urging me closer, Gavin helped me from my seat and straight into his lap. I parted my thighs, bringing my center directly in line with his groin where I could feel a firm bulge trapped between us. He was hard.

I let out a gentle moan of approval, and Gavin's mouth pulled into a crooked smile. The expression on his face was perfectly controlled, but the steady strum of the pulse in his neck signaled his excitement.

"I can feel how hot and wet you are through your dress."

I was sure my cheeks were stained red, and was thankful for our dim surroundings.

"Is that for me?" he asked.

I bit my lower lip, fairly certain his question was rhetorical.

He knew it was, and he shook his head. "Naughty girl."

He was right. I couldn't believe what had come over me. We were parked on a hillside, and the driver was mere feet away. Since this wasn't a stretch limo, there was no partition, no barrier between the driver and us. But damn if I was going to let that stop me. I hungered for Gavin's touch like I'd never craved anything before.

It started out as a dirty little secret, something to amuse myself with. I lived a boring existence—work, home, bed . . . and Gavin was a distraction. Maybe I should have left it there, but I hadn't.

And here I was.

His punishing mouth on mine.

His hands in my hair.

My heart in my throat.

The firmness of his erection pressing between my thighs.

And my mind reeling with what might come next.

Chapter Thirteen

Gavin

The desire to ravage Emma was almost overwhelming. I didn't know what kind of spell this demure little thing in my lap had put me under.

There was no denying she was my type, sure. And the little moan she'd let out had almost sent me straight to my knees. But still . . .

Control was my middle name. Yet right now? Every ounce of my resolve had been pushed to the limit.

Despite all my years of practice, I felt like a horny teenager, ready to paw at the first girl to show me her bra.

This was the exact reason I hadn't brought her home. It was much too private, too intimate.

I wouldn't let anything happen in front of Ben. At least, that's what I'd told myself when we left the gala. Yet here we were. My steely will had all but disappeared, and Emma was writhing in my lap, making soft, need-filled sounds that pulsed straight to my cock.

Breaking away from the kiss, Emma gripped the

lapels of my jacket and tried to shove it down my shoulders. I doubted she noticed the way I flinched when she touched me, but still, I couldn't allow it to happen again.

"Hands behind your back, pet," I said as coolly and calmly as I could manage.

Emma obeyed, crossing her wrists and placing them at her lower back. The position thrust her beautiful tits up and out, and that was all it took to destroy the thin strands of my self-control.

Suddenly, I didn't care about Ben or how I'd wanted things to go. All I wanted was to get inside her.

After untying the knot at the back of her neck that secured her dress in place, I started to peel it away.

"Wait."

I raised a brow as she clutched the material to her chest.

"Can't he ... see us?" she whispered, nodding toward Ben.

Glancing ahead, I shrugged. "Trust me. He's not

watching. He's paid very well for his discretion."

She hesitated, softening in my lap, and made my cock twitch again.

"If he did glance back here, all he'd see was your bare back. You're facing me," I added.

She nodded, and I felt the last of her resistance slip away.

I lowered the straps of her dress and freed the most mouthwatering set of breasts I'd ever seen.

"I don't think we'll be needing this." Unclasping the simple nude-colored bra she wore, I tossed it on the seat beside us. Her lingerie wasn't sexy, wasn't something meant to entice or thrill, but my pulse jackhammered all the same as I took in her rosy nipples, stiff and waiting for me.

Testing the weight of her breasts in my hands, I let slip a groan of approval, and Emma sucked in a sharp inhale.

At first, I kneaded her tender flesh, stroking her nipples gently with my thumbs as I savored the image of her body in the moonlight. But even I knew, after all this time? All this tension? It wasn't enough. Her body was begging for more, and I gave her what she needed, plucking her tight buds between my fingers until they hardened, and Emma cried out.

Lowering my mouth to her skin, I trailed my tongue along her cleavage, her collarbone, only venturing lower when she made a frustrated sound of need.

Sucking the firm peaks into my mouth, I worked my tongue over each one. I wanted to see if I could make her come like this, but I was too needy for her scent, to feel her wet heat on my skin.

She squirmed against my cock, forcing a ragged breath from my lungs. I wanted nothing more than to bury myself inside her.

Pulling the skirt of her dress up around her hips, Emma shifted, allowing me access to the damp scrap of lace she wore. With a twist of my fingers, it was out of my way.

Rocking her hips forward, Emma showed me a peek of swollen pink flesh that made my mouth water. As I swept my thumb across her firm clit, she made a soft whimper of pleasure.

I loved how responsive she was, but this this was hardly the time or place. "Stay nice and quiet for me, okay?"

She bit her lip and gave me a tight nod.

Kissing her eager mouth, I swallowed the cries and mewls of pleasure I coaxed from her with skilled fingers.

There was something about this woman that made me want to put her on her knees and dominate her, shove my length down her throat until she gagged. But that would come with time. For tonight, this was all about Emma.

"You're not used to this?" I asked, though I tried to mask my concern.

She shook her head. "I've only been with two men. Neither was . . ."

She stopped and I shot her a questioning look. She wanted me to fill in the blank. Experienced? Demanding? I wasn't sure. But the desire to protect her and pleasure her warred with me.

"Don't worry. This will feel good." Sweeping my fingers through her arousal, I enjoyed the way she shuddered and shifted in my lap, rocking herself closer.

Pushing two fingers inside her, I felt her tense. I kissed her again and let her adjust. As I carefully slid my thick fingers out and then pushed in again, Emma closed her eyes, rolling her hips along with my thrusts.

The light streaming through the moon roof provided the perfect view, and I couldn't resist watching her face in awe as I worked her over. "Does that feel good?"

She pressed a kiss to my lips, murmuring a soft, "Yes, very."

"You are so fucking tight. I can't even imagine how good you'd feel riding my cock."

That dirty remark earned me another moan of approval, and a wet coating of her cream on my fingers.

"Ride my fingers. Make yourself come."

At first, I thought I had pegged her wrong—maybe she wasn't the type to follow orders.

Then relief sagged in her shoulders, like she'd been

waiting for me to give her permission all along.

She moved her hips up and down, rocking against my hand. Slowly at first, and then as I curled my fingers forward and found the tender spot inside, she moved faster.

"That's it," I murmured. She was coming undone and I fucking loved it. Far more than I should have.

With each thrust, she took me deeper, and the soft sound of her damp arousal was the most beautiful sound in the world.

Emma's tight body clamped down on me, her head dropping back between her shoulders as she came in a rush of wet heat that coated my fingers and made my cock jerk hard against my zipper.

Removing my hand from between her legs, I inspected my glistening fingers in the dim light. Her scent was light and sweet, and I wanted to taste it. But even more than that, I wanted to make her squirm.

Wiping the sticky mess she'd made onto the leg of my pants, which were already ruined, I made a low *tsking* sound in my throat. "Look at what you've done."

Emma's eyes widened as she moved from my lap to the seat beside me.

"These pants are positively ruined."

"I'm sorry. Can I . . . ?" Emma reached for the bulge still raging in my pants, but I batted her hand away. "Don't you want me to—"

I shook my head. "We need to be getting back. It's late."

The excuse sounded lame even to my ears, but I knew if I let her touch me now, I would explode. I needed to get home, to manage this need myself before things got out of hand.

And I could only imagine what Emma must be thinking.

"Ben," I barked out. "Proceed to Emma's address."

The limo rolled forward, pulling onto the semicircular drive that led to the road beyond.

Emma watched me from the corner of her eye as we drove. I knew she was probably thinking she'd done something wrong, but that couldn't be further from the truth. I'd never wanted a woman more.

The silent drive passed by slowly, and when we finally pulled to a stop in front of her brownstone, Emma got out of the limo without a word, her shoulders sagging and her chin tucked into her chest.

I exited behind her and escorted her to the door. It was almost midnight, but I felt so keyed up and on edge, I knew sleep wouldn't come easily tonight.

"Is everything ... okay?" she asked. "Did I do something wrong?"

I leaned in and pressed a kiss to her mouth. "Everything's fine. Good night, Miss Bell."

"Good night, Gavin."

"My assistant will be in touch with you when I have another event I need an escort for." It was cold, even to my ears, but I didn't know how to make it sound any different. It had always been the way I operated.

With a flash of anger in her bright gaze, Emma turned for the door and headed inside, closing it firmly behind her. I stayed until I heard the lock turn and then headed back to the limo.

"Where to, Mr. Kingsley?" Ben asked.

Knowing sleep was a long way off, I weighed my options. Though the idea of jerking one out appealed to me greatly, I couldn't bring myself to go home to an empty house.

"Take me to the office."

Despite it being after eleven at night, the lamp in Quinn's office was still lit, and I bypassed my own office in favor of his.

His social skills were worse than mine—if that were even possible—but still, it surprised me he wasn't out somewhere, or at least relaxing at home.

"Gavin? That you?" he called out.

He must have heard my footsteps approaching down the hall. I could have laughed at the fact he didn't even consider that it might be Cooper.

"What are you still doing here?" I asked, rounding the corner to his office. I found him seated behind his desk, a glass of bourbon in front of him.

"I could ask you the same." He smirked. Dark circles

rested beneath his eyes, and his hair was overdue for a cut. In short, he looked like shit.

I knew he worked too much, knew he shouldered too much of the responsibility around here. But it had always been that way. Quinn was barely two years older than me, but he took the older-brother shit seriously. Growing up, he'd always looked out for me. Shit, he looked out for everyone. He had a soft spot in his heart for prostitutes and escorts. He'd saved more than one girl from life on the streets, and protected those who worked for us fiercely. Even though we didn't always see eye to eye on everything, he was a good man.

"I was just going over last quarter's financial statements." He closed his eyes and pressed his fingers to his temples.

"Everything good?" I asked, helping myself to a glass of his bourbon before taking a seat in front of his desk.

"Everything's good," he confirmed, closing his laptop.

I sensed there was something else going on, some other reason he was here right now, but I didn't press him.

Quinn took another slow sip of his drink, watching me. "Why are you here? Did you forget something?"

I shook my head. "Just wanted to check on a few things." The lie rolled easily off my tongue, but my brother knew me better than to believe it. He didn't have to say as much—I could see it in his eyes. He saw right through me.

"Tonight was your evening out with Emma, wasn't it?" His dark brows drew together as he continued to study me.

"It was. I just dropped her off at home." Taking another long sip of my drink, I hoped he read my *fuck off* signal loud and clear.

"How did that go? Did she live up to expectations?"

No such luck.

I shrugged. Maybe he thought I fucked her. I obviously didn't. Ben could vouch for that. *Jesus.* "It was fine. We went to the event, and then I took her home. I won the Seychelles trip this year."

"Oh, good. Another overpriced vacation you'll never go on. Don't change the subject."

I rolled my eyes, adding another measure of bourbon to both our glasses. The bastard was referring to the trip to Tahiti I never took. Not that it went to waste. I gifted it to our highest-earning girl last year. She took her parents. I still had the photo of them on lounge chairs sitting on my desk.

As much as I didn't want Quinn's advice right now, I knew he was about to dish up a heaping serving. I bit the inside of my cheek and waited. The dude clearly had something he needed to get off his chest.

"Something's different with this one," he said. "I'm just trying to put my finger on what it is."

He'd figure it out eventually; it didn't take a rocket scientist. I drank the rest of my bourbon, waiting.

"I'm just trying to figure out if it's more than just the fact she looks like Ashley."

Ding, ding, ding.

Fucker.

"Drop it, Quinn. It has nothing to do with that."

I didn't want it to, and honestly, as I got to know

Emma, the less their similarities seemed to matter. That first time I saw her in the coffee shop, though, I'd been knocked back three years.

Looking at Emma was like staring into the face of my once-upon-a-time. But I knew that wasn't possible. I'd been there the day they'd lowered her into the ground. I'd said my good-byes, as final as they were.

They shared a few similar features, but Emma was her own woman, and one I was quickly becoming fascinated with.

"I know there's something different about her. You haven't even looked twice at a woman in months. Just be careful this time."

I rose to my feet, my blood pumping fast. "Don't you think I fucking know that?"

The fucking kicker? Quinn was right. Emma was feisty, yet had all the leanings of a submissive, which I'd always been attracted to.

"I don't want this to end badly," Quinn added.

Rubbing my temples, I regretted ever coming into the office tonight. Jacking off alone in the shower would have been much better.

"If you're through, I'm tired. I'm going to head home."

"Didn't mean to piss you off," Quinn said as I headed out of his office.

"Don't worry about it," I called over my shoulder, not bothering to look back.

As fucked up as all this was, I knew it was only going to get more complicated.

Tonight's foreplay wasn't nearly enough to satisfy the beast inside me. I wanted the pretty little Emma Bell. And I was going to have her.

Chapter Fourteen

Emma

I stared down at the article's title in a bold font: "How to Make Your Man Beg for More." Rolling my eyes, I shoved the vinyl-covered magazine back into its resting place on the periodical shelf.

I couldn't even make Gavin take what I was offering, let alone beg. And I still couldn't help the hot shame that burned deep inside my chest when I thought about the way he'd swatted my hands away from him.

What kind of man didn't want to come?

I ran my fingers through my hair. That was just . . . insane.

Things had gotten so intense in his limo. With my dress pooled around my waist and my panties soaked through, he'd done such naughty things to my body, made me want things I hadn't in a very long time.

I'd never been a sexual creature, never lusted after someone the way my favorite authors described in some of the romance novels I loved. For a long time, I'd thought that was what Nathan wished would change so badly. Like, if I could just get that switch in my brain to flick on, everything would be okay again.

Not that things had ever been okay between us. Not really.

And now, after years of my trying and wishing and wanting to change, Gavin had turned me into a whimpering, writhing mess. But worse than that? He apparently wasn't interested. After all those years of wanting to be someone else, to act like a real woman, I had unlocked my own sexuality just to have it thrown back in my face.

It was possible that it had nothing to do with me, but I knew better than that. Whatever his deal was, Gavin didn't want me to touch him, didn't want me to pleasure him the way he had done to me.

All night, I'd racked my brain, trying to figure out if it was me, or maybe Cooper, or maybe something else entirely that had made things so strained between us. I wanted to understand and, in a way, I think I did.

Just as I had a desire to please and to be taken, he desired total control.

I'd never been so turned on in my entire life. It was as though we shared a secret sexual connection. His need to possess matched perfectly with my need to be taken. And if he'd have asked? I would have given it to him. Everything.

In the days that followed, I couldn't help but wonder about what that meant, and why I felt so alive in his presence, despite all my experience screaming at me to run away and go for the safer, sweeter option. Did we have a touch of the Dominant/submissive leanings I'd only read about in my favorite erotic novels? The rough edge of his voice, the intensity of the moment . . . it was almost unspoken between us, but oh so perfect. It sparked me to life in ways I couldn't begin to comprehend.

I would have thought, after everything I'd been through with Nathan, that I would tear away from the idea of someone possessing me again. But then, maybe my past was exactly what was driving me to experiment?

These new, sweetly dark fantasies were something to fill the void of heartache and terror that had been my love life before. And if I could manage it? Well, then I would prove to myself that I could have a satisfying sexual relationship and not lose myself, that the real control was always with me.

And so I spent days waffling—at war with myself over what should have or might have or could have happened. But in the end, I figured out a few essential truths.

I wouldn't let my fears over what happened with Nathan stop me from living my life. This was the most important thing, something I'd reminded myself of every day since I'd finally gotten away from him.

But also? I wanted Gavin. Rough and dominating and all wrong for me, and all I wanted was more.

I could tell myself whatever I wanted, but my heart knew the truth. I needed to feel as alive as I had in his arms that night. I needed to feel like a free, sexual, and capable woman.

When Monday came and I still had no word from either Kingsley brother, I decided to take matters into my own hands. With a deep breath, I fished my phone from my desk drawer and opened a message to Gavin.

Before I could get out more than four words,

though, my phone pinged and my heart leaped into my throat. Maybe Gavin knew I was thinking of him. That we had some strange connection.

But it wasn't Gavin. It was Cooper, and it read simply, *Lunch at the office?*

Easy, happy Cooper. The safe choice, the guy I should want.

"Be there in ten," I typed back, then grabbed my purse and stuffed my phone inside.

With a thirty-minute lunch break, I'd never make it. I slouched my shoulders and stood in Stan's doorway. "I've got a 'lady errand' to run."

Stan nodded quickly. "Of course. Do what you need to do."

I tried to stifle my smile as I walked calmly out of the library and hopped on the train. I didn't know if this lunch would be with Gavin and Cooper both, but the fact was that the idea of seeing either brother made my heart leap and my pulse tick.

When I got to the main floor of their office building, I let myself inside.

"Afternoon." Sonja watched me as I entered, and I was hoping that her sneer was only in my imagination.

Turning the corner, I made my way to Cooper's door and knocked lightly. He wasn't there, so I walked farther down the hall, toward where I could see half of a tall, muscled man in a navy suit.

"Hey." The man turned. It was Cooper, calling to me from the doorway to Gavin's office.

Hell.

And also, yes.

I felt a pang of guilt looking at Cooper's stunning body and thinking back to Gavin's expert fingers.

"Let's get going."

I heard Gavin's gruff voice before I saw him. My self-doubt returned instantly, but luckily, as I walked inside the massive room, my grumbling stomach drew my attention to the impressive lunch spread on the large conference table in the center of Gavin's office.

I swallowed hard, looking for a plate to serve myself, and my gaze fell on Quinn, who was seated at the other end of the table, completing the overwhelmingly handsome trio.

"Hey," Quinn said. "Nice to see you again.

I nodded. "Likewise."

"We ordered you a salad." Cooper signaled me to my seat where a large mixed-green salad with all the fixings waited for me.

Gavin cleared his throat and started in a rough, to-the-point tone. "Upcoming schedules," he said, his hazel gaze glancing from me to his brothers as I took my seat in front of him. An untouched plate sat in front of him.

"Have a little class, Gavin," Quinn said. "Let her get settled. We invited her for lunch, not the inquisition." Then, turning to me, he added, "Would you like something to drink before we get started?"

Why couldn't I be into at least one of the two sweet brothers? Of course, Gavin being short with me drove me even harder to want to please him.

"Water is fine, thanks." I gave Quinn a quick smile, and he pushed a water bottle toward me while I used the plastic fork to stab a bite of salad. Apparently, I was the only one eating.

"There. Was that so hard?" Quinn muttered to Gavin, whose mouth was nothing more than a thin line.

"A healthy appetite. I love that." Cooper smiled as I dug into my salad, and I watched Gavin grimace at him.

That's right, Mr. Don't-touch-me-there.

"Keeping my energy up." I winked at Cooper, then popped a cherry tomato into my mouth and kept from looking at Gavin directly.

Gavin cleared his throat. "We want to work out our upcoming schedules."

"To avoid any conflicts," Cooper added.

I looked to Gavin to see his nostrils flare.

"I have a gallery opening tomorrow night, and a golf outing the next day," Cooper started.

I nodded along, glancing from Cooper to Quinn as Cooper went on. Still, the longer I refused eye contact with Gavin, the more I could feel him staring at me, making my skin heat.

I tried my best to focus on my lunch and listen to the

dizzying conversation by these three distracting men.

A few moments later, there was a soft knock on the door and Alyssa popped her head in and looked at Gavin. "Sorry to interrupt, sir. There's a telephone call for you, and it's urgent."

Gavin nodded. "Be right there."

She smiled big and looked right at me for a moment before directing her attention to Gavin once again. "Sorry, I wouldn't interrupt if it wasn't urgent."

Gavin cleared his throat before he stood and followed her.

"I've got to run too. It was lovely to see you again, Emma." Quinn tipped an imaginary hat at me, and I smiled and tipped an imaginary hat back at him.

Cooper and I remained sitting in Gavin's office. I finally allowed myself to relax under the warmth of Cooper's gaze.

"How are you doing, princess? Can you handle the schedule?"

Alyssa appeared again in the doorway before I had a

chance to reply. "Gavin had to step out. He'll call you to fill you in, Cooper." She seemed pleased with herself as she shut the door to the office, leaving us alone in the space that smelled too much like Gavin.

His voice played back in my head on a loop. *Naughty girl.* I wondered if he'd used the same words with other women, if he took them on similar dates in his limo with Ben in the front seat.

Huffing out a deep sigh, I tried to forget what had happened in the back seat. I pushed my salad away on the table, no longer hungry.

"That bad, huh?" Cooper asked. He was so handsome and sweet.

"To be honest, it's all a little overwhelming."

I loved that I could tell Cooper how I was feeling. Gavin might be a walking sex bomb, but he was also cocky and rude. The more I thought about it, the more I wanted to tell him he could keep his thousand dollars. I'd rather have my self-respect. And given my past, I didn't trust myself around men like him.

Maybe it was time to move on and forget this ever

happened. Maybe I didn't need this shit. Maybe I could say I'd only go on dates with Cooper.

But, who was I kidding? Gavin would haunt my dreams if I didn't see this through to the end.

Cooper would never take control like that. He was too . . . what was the word? Polite, respectful? Did that mean that Gavin wasn't those things? The evidence that I was repeating an unhealthy pattern was mounting.

"Does that mean you're out?" Cooper asked, and though his face was impassive, I knew the answer meant a lot to him.

I shook my head, much to my own surprise. "No. I'm going to make it work. I do need to get going though. I told my coworkers I was running an errand."

Cooper smiled and walked me to the door. I stepped out onto the busy sidewalk and noticed a woman glaring at me. Maybe she knew what these offices were for, even though there was no name on the door.

"Emma."

I heard my name and turned to see Gavin standing on the curb in front of the building.

"What are you doing here? I thought you left," I said, butterflies exploding into flight in my belly.

"Damn drivers. Ben is out today, unfortunately."

The mention of Ben instantly brought me back to the limo. I could feel my cheeks burning, which earned me a smile from Gavin for the first time today. I tried to swallow the lump building in my throat.

"Oh, well, see you later." I turned to walk away but Gavin grabbed my wrist, pulling me back toward him.

"What's wrong, little minx?"

I tried to find the words offensive instead of arousing. It didn't work.

"What happened in the limo ..." My mouth went dry, and I still wasn't sure if I wanted to ask him for round two or if I ought to tell him it could never happen again. For Cooper's sake. For the sake of my ever-dwindling dignity.

"You rode my fingers," he said quite loudly.

A man passing by on the sidewalk whipped his head in our direction.

"You wouldn't let me touch *you*, though." I whispered the words.

Gavin grinned. "Touching me is a privilege you have to earn." He stroked his fingertips down my bare arms. "But you're mine to play with, so I can touch you anytime I want."

I let out a small gasp, feeling breathless at his words. What arrogance, and yet I wanted to earn it. I wanted him to touch me anytime he wanted to.

When I said nothing, warring with myself, he pulled me closer still. God, I loved the feel of him. And damn it if this didn't make me a whore, but the library was truthfully on the brink of closure. After the hard winter last year, the roof was leaking so badly, we had buckets collecting water. A crew was already hard at work repairing it because of Gavin's donation. If it weren't for him, I might not have either of my two jobs at this point.

Still, that didn't give him the right to toy with me.

"Look, Gavin, I really appreciate what you've done for me . . ." I started a speech of protest, but he pulled me in close. I could feel the heat from him.

"What's wrong? Scared you that you liked it rough?" His hot breath fanned my cheek, and I shivered despite myself.

My head swam, and I fought to find the words to describe how I felt. I couldn't answer because he wasn't wrong, and I wasn't willing to give him the satisfaction of a yes.

"I . . ."

Gavin put his finger to my lips to stop me.

A black town car pulled up in front of us at the curb, and the driver stepped out. "Mr. Kingsley?"

Cooper burst through the building's door at the same moment and looked right at us, huddled close together. He lifted his hand in a small wave to me before turning to walk down the street.

"I've got to go," Gavin said plainly, and like a switch, the magic was gone and the asshole was back, leaving me alone, staring after him.

The sense of shame washed over me again and stuck with me as I sat alone on the dirty train, jerking back and forth as we snaked back toward the musty library.

Back to reality. Back to my mundane, boring life. And in that moment, I knew I wouldn't say no. Not to Gavin.

Not to anything he asked of me.

Chapter Fifteen

Gavin

"What the fuck are you two up to?" Quinn's assessing gaze darted between Cooper and me.

The hum of the air-conditioning in Quinn's office was the only source of distraction. It was the end of the day, and ever since Emma strutted out of the office at midday, the day had dragged by at a snail's pace.

"Whatever do you mean, brother dearest?" Cooper asked, a smirk on his lips.

"This pissing match." Quinn waved his hand between us. "One of you needs to fuck her and get this over with."

Cooper's nostrils flared, and he looked like he was ready to punch something. I felt the same way.

"Don't see how that will help," I muttered under my breath.

"Then lay claim to her. End this bullshit arrangement. Admit you want her in your life," Cooper taunted. "I'll back off."

That wasn't going to happen. At least, not while I still had my wits about me.

"Not everything ends in death and devastation. Sometimes there are happily-ever-afters," Quinn said. "Or so I've heard." He forced a smile, and for a second, I wondered if even he believed the shit coming out of his mouth.

"And when has any of us experienced anything close to that?" I barked.

My brothers stayed silent.

"Exactly. Never."

"Doesn't mean it couldn't happen," Quinn said.

"Drop it, asshole," I warned.

Quinn rose to his feet, hefting out a sigh as though rising from the chair took a great amount of effort. He suddenly looked much older than his thirty-six years. "Don't let it affect your work."

"Lecture over yet, Dad?" Cooper asked.

"Long as you two can behave like goddamn adults, yes."

"You need to ask Gavin about that," Cooper said, crumpling his water bottle and tossing it across the room in a perfect arch to land in the wastebasket.

I rolled my eyes. Lately I felt like I couldn't do or say anything without facing their scrutiny. Things weren't always this way. We used to stay out of each other's way, and we used to mind our own fucking business.

God, how I missed those days. It seemed like everything had changed, and I was exhausted. Maybe I should take one of those vacations Quinn was always suggesting. Then again, maybe not. Who knew what Cooper would get into while I was gone. Rather not what, but who. That thought shouldn't bother me so much, yet it undeniably did.

"Just want to be sure you two know what the fuck you're doing," Quinn added.

"Everything's fine, Quinn. No need to pull the concerned-older-brother act." I forced a grin, but it felt more like a grimace. I wasn't sure what had me so on edge. Actually, I was one-hundred percent sure her initials were E.B., but I was trying to ignore that fact.

"Good." Quinn nodded. "I just don't want anything getting in the way of running the business. We can't afford mistakes."

"I quite agree. But, seriously, it's all good." Cooper rose to his feet and placed one hand on my shoulder. "Right, brother?"

I nodded.

Our meeting was over, and since I had a client meeting to prepare for, I tried to force all thoughts of Emma out of my brain. It was easier said than done.

Sonja knocked on the frame of my open door. Letting herself inside, she set a stack of manila folders on my desk. "Cooper did very well at the gala. We have three new client requests."

"That's great." I sifted through the folders. A politician, a professional athlete, and some dude I'd never heard of.

"There's something else . . . and I wasn't sure how you'd want me to handle it."

Was that . . . hesitation? Sonja never hesitated. But here she was, biting her bottom lip and looking at me like she had to deliver the world's worst medical prognosis. She managed the office and handled all client and escort relations.

My curiosity piqued, I slid into my desk chair, watching her. "What is it?"

Sonja lowered herself into the chair in front of me. "A client has requested Emma specifically."

I shook my head, ignoring the pulse that suddenly jackhammered in my neck. "She's not even in the database. How's that possible?"

She cleared her throat. "He met her at the event with Cooper. Wondered if she was available to attend a wedding with him in Scotland next month."

Ignoring the sudden ache in my temples that meant a headache was coming, I shifted in my seat. "That's . . . no. The answer is no. She's not available for hire."

She nodded. "That's what I told him. I knew it was some type of private arrangement between you and Cooper, and I don't mean to pry, but do you really think that's wise?"

My temples now full-on throbbing, I took a deep breath. "What do you mean?"

"Sir, I hope you forgive me if I'm overstepping, but ever since Emma's sudden entrance into your lives, things between you and Cooper have been different."

Fuck. So, it wasn't just Quinn being an asshole. Sonja had noticed it too.

Trying to maintain my composure, I asked, "What do you mean?"

Again, she hesitated. "If she's become a distraction, maybe it's best to let her go."

I blinked. In all the time Sonja had worked with me, she'd never said a single thing about any of the girls. Not when they failed to show up on dates, not when they quit without notice. Never.

"You were all for hiring her," I said, tilting my head. "Why the sudden change of heart?"

Why would she care if Cooper and I were having some secret competition with the pretty newcomer?

"I don't want her to cause any issues between you and Cooper, that's all. Things have shifted. We can all feel it," she said, her voice growing softer.

"Sonja, when have you ever known my brother and I to let a woman come between us?"

"There's a first time for everything." Sonja raised a perfectly plucked eyebrow at me, and I could have laughed if it weren't for the serious tone to this conversation.

I reached across the desk and patted the top of her hand. "This is just business. There's no need to worry."

"I do worry about you. All of you, but you especially, Gavin. Ever since . . ."

"Don't," I warned. The next person to bring up her name was getting throat-punched. I didn't care that Sonja had a vagina. I'd reached my limit on this personal, prying bullshit today.

She straightened her skirt. "All I'm saying is that if you needed a plus-one for an event, all you had to do was ask."

I blinked again, for the first time in my life not sure what to say. Finally, I settled on, "I already ask too much of you."

Watching her sit across from me, I studied Sonja for the first time in a long time—maybe ever. Dressed in a tailored skirt suit, with shoulder-length wavy blond hair, she was an attractive, vibrant woman. I recalled from her birthday earlier this year that she had just recently turned thirty-nine, though she didn't look it. I couldn't help but wonder if she'd wasted her prime years working long hours to help my brothers and me get our business off the ground.

If she didn't work so much, would she be married by now? Maybe even have a little one at home? Probably. I wondered if that was what she wanted. Sonja never talked about her personal life. And despite working long hours beside her, I realized that I didn't actually know her very well.

"I care about you too much to drag you into my shit," I said.

"I'm here, and the offer stands. Whatever you need."

Sonja couldn't possibly understand my needs. And if she did? she wouldn't volunteer herself so quickly.

"Besides, Quinn would have my balls if something ever happened between us that made you not want to work here anymore. You're too valuable to this place. You keep us all sane."

She smiled and rose to her feet. "Okay."

I watched her head for the door, hoping I'd merely imagined the odd tension buzzing between us. I had more of that than I could handle already with the distracting Miss Bell.

"As long as you're good with everything, then so am I." She turned and shot me a distracted smile. "I've got to go. Cooper asked me to send Emma a new dress for the next event, and I don't want to forget."

With that, she sailed out of the room leaving me staring after her, irritated and a little proud at the same time. Sonja was smart and savvy enough to see through my ruse, and had let loose one final arrow before parting.

One that landed full-on center mass and stayed lodged there all fucking day as I sat and seethed, imagining the sensual creation Emma would be wearing for my brother.

Son of a bitch.

Chapter Sixteen

Emma

Another beautiful dress arrived at my front door the following morning, green and lacy and backless. A note attached read:

Princess, you'll be the most exquisite work of art in the gallery tonight.

— Cooper

Not for the first time, I wondered how he'd felt when he'd seen Gavin and me huddled together outside the office building. Each time I thought of Cooper's small wave, another roll of guilt took hold of me, and I had to sit down and breathe deeply before I could focus again.

The truth was that neither of these men ought to be attached to me. I shouldn't be the one worried about whether I was getting between them, because this had been a deal of their own design. If Gavin wanted to do . . . well, all the things he wanted to do to me, it shouldn't matter to Cooper.

But what if it did?

I could never forgive myself for hurting someone as sweet and charming and nice as Cooper. By rights, he was the sort of man I should have been focused on. And the way he'd kissed me, so tender and delicate? There was a sort of passion there too, wasn't there?

Now, in addition to all my worries and concerns about the house and Gavin and the library, I added Cooper to the list. If I didn't sort things out, and soon, I was going to give myself an ulcer. But I had no time to worry about that.

By the time afternoon came, I was slipping into my dress and fussing with my hair, getting ready for another night with the man who should have been my perfect match.

When Cooper arrived, things went as smoothly as they had during our last date. We fell into easy conversation—the scene with Gavin ignored but not forgotten—and time flew as we headed to the party. Cooper really was sweet and sexy all rolled into one captivating package. In many ways, I knew he would be perfect for me, but the more I realized that, the more I craved the intense connection I shared with the dominating and enigmatic Gavin. The thought made my stomach twist, and not in the butterfly way.

Soon, the limo was dropping us off on the charming Newbury Street in front of the art gallery. There were only a dozen people or so in the small gallery space enjoying wine and cheese.

"Are we early?" I asked.

Cooper chuckled in response and led me through the doorway.

"Good evening, Mr. Kingsley." A woman wearing all black with a short blond bob walked eagerly toward Cooper and completely ignored me. I could almost see the dollar signs in her eyes. Cooper gave her his most charming smile.

"Right this way, please." The woman led us behind a curtain to a back room with a spiral staircase. "They're all down there."

"After you, princess," Cooper said, blowing a kiss in the blonde's direction as a thank-you.

"Former fling of yours?" I raised my eyebrows as we

descended the staircase into the darkness below.

Cooper laughed. "She's gay. No worries, I'm all yours."

Another twinge of guilt coursed through me, but I ignored it as we stepped into the dimly lit basement of the gallery. My eyes began to adjust and two dozen or more faces appeared in the semi-darkness.

Most of the guests were well-dressed men in expensive tailored suits, though a few were women in dresses as fancy as my own. Not one of the women looked a day older than thirty.

Are these all escorts? Does everyone here know that I'm an escort?

Thinking of myself as an escort was still strange. It felt much more like a friendly outing, beside the fact, of course, that he was paying me to be here.

"Can I get you a drink?" Cooper asked.

"Yes, please." Tonight, I could use the break from my own thoughts.

Cooper headed to a small table in the corner and

grabbed two small glasses of clear liquid, each with what appeared to be a slice of pickle at the bottom. My nostrils burned at the smell.

"Is this vodka?" I wrinkled my nose.

Cooper nodded. "With a pickle back." He drank the shot quickly and then set his glass on the table between us.

I exhaled sharply and followed his lead, only to come up coughing at the intense flavor of pure alcohol.

Cooper laughed and took the glass from me. "You okay?"

A tall, silver-haired man approached us. "Cooper Kingsley?"

"Bruce, great to see you."

The men exchanged a firm handshake.

"And who is this beauty?" Bruce asked him, eying me up and down greedily. "When can I take you out, gorgeous?"

"This is Emma, my girlfriend. Sorry, Bruce. Can you grab us a couple more drinks, babe?"

Cooper smiled at me sweetly. I nodded and left the pair of men who huddled to talk in a low whisper.

The table was filled with more of the vodka-and-pickle drinks. I grabbed another and downed it before bringing two back over to Cooper, who stood talking to another man. I watched the sly passing of the business cards as I brought back the drinks.

"Tying one on tonight?" Cooper said as I handed him the drink. He raised his glass to clink it against mine, and we drained our drinks.

"These grow on you." I was already slurring and Cooper chuckled, placing his hand around my waist and pulling me close to him. He felt so much like Gavin, and smelled like him too. I thought drinking was supposed to get your mind off of things.

"So, I'm your girlfriend now, huh? This is news to me." I raised my eyebrows at him.

"It's easier than explaining that Gavin and I share you as our own private escort, right?" Cooper grinned, clearly pleased with himself.

I nodded. "Another drink?"

His eyes went wide as a mischievous smile tugged at his lips and his dimple flashed. "You've got it."

Soon, he returned with two more glasses, and I downed the liquid quickly again. I no longer needed to cough at the taste. The heat of the alcohol raced through me.

"Should we look at the art for a little while?" he asked.

"Where is it?" I looked around the dim room again, but there wasn't anything hanging on the walls.

"This way." Cooper led me toward the end of the room where a crowd was standing in front of what must have been the art. I looked at it, but only vaguely as my vision had started to blur a little. Another few minutes passed, and I realized with a snort-laugh that was beginning to lose my balance in my high heels.

"Are you tipping the room to the side?" I demanded in a stage whisper, closing one eye as I tried to get Cooper back into focus.

He caught me by the elbow as I stumbled and chuckled. "I see we have ourselves a lightweight. Okay, princess, I think we need to get you out of here."

A poorly timed hiccup made him chuckle again and had me grinning along with him.

Cooper. Easy-peasy Cooper. No drama. No fear or shame. It was . . . nice. Just like him.

I sighed and nestled closer as he took out his phone and typed out a quick message. His screen pinged back almost instantly.

"All right, the limo's out front."

Cooper followed me up the stairs, one hand on my back steadying me. He was probably getting an eyeful of my ass or the bare skin of the backless dress he'd picked out for me, but I couldn't find it in me to mind. He held me close to him as I stumbled toward the door, feeling the effects of the vodka more intensely as we stepped into the light.

By the time we got in the limo, I was in a haze. The swaying of the car wasn't helping. Cooper led me out when we stopped, and I looked around to see he hadn't taken me home.

"Where are we?"

"My place in Cambridge." Cooper shot me a sweet half smile and continued. "I'm going to take care of you, get you sobered up before I can take you home in good conscience. Wanted to make sure you were going to be okay, princess. You had three shots in a short time, and that was on my watch. I didn't realize how hard it would hit you."

I nodded, my alcohol-soaked brain taking in the massive ornate building.

"Good evening, Mr. Kingsley." A man in a red-and-gold bellhop uniform greeted us as we moved toward the elevator.

Cooper pressed the button for the top floor, number fifteen. The elevator rose fast, and I stumbled again. Cooper caught me, holding me close during the ride up. Soon, the doors opened into a small vestibule containing a single door.

I tried to keep steady and hold on to my thoughts, the ones swirling around madly, telling me this was nuts. That I should turn around and go home before something happened I might regret. But I couldn't seem to catch hold of a single one.

"I think I need a hot shower and some coffee," I mumbled.

The next second, Cooper swept me into his house and I went, closing the door behind me, the click echoing like a shot.

Chapter Seventeen

Cooper

"How are you feeling?" I helped Emma through the front door and held her forearm as she slipped off her high heels.

"Mmm, good." She nodded more eagerly than necessary, like she was trying hard to convince me. I knew she was drunk, and I felt bad for introducing her to my favorite vodka. "It's freezing in here, though." She wrapped her arms around herself, shivering in her pretty emerald lace dress.

"Yeah. Sorry about that." Every woman I'd ever brought home complained about the exact same thing. It appeared the fairer sex didn't appreciate my fondness for sixty-six-degree air-conditioning. It was a luxury I grew up without, and I now tended to overindulge. "Hang tight. I'll get you a sweatshirt."

I left Emma roaming through the oversized foyer, admiring the art that hung on the walls, and headed to the master bedroom.

"And turn up the heat," she shouted from behind

me.

"Yes, ma'am."

Moments later, I handed her my softest gray sweatshirt.

"Harvard?" she asked, pushing her arms through the oversized sleeves.

I shook my head. "I didn't go there, if that's what you're wondering. Didn't have the money. Or the grades for college."

"Did you want to go?"

"Of course."

"You could," she said, nodding at me. "Go back now."

I shrugged. "I'm twenty-eight, and I do well for myself. There's really no need now."

As I spoke, Emma wandered around my loft, acquainting herself with the space. Trailing her fingertips along the exposed-brick wall in the living room, she stopped at the wall of windows that led out to the balcony.

"You can see everything from here," she said.

Sliding up behind her, I placed my hands on her waist. I told myself it was just to steady her, but it really was only an excuse to touch her. She looked damn cute in her formal gown and my favorite sweatshirt.

Emma turned to face me. Her eyes were full of questions, and in that moment, I wished I had all the answers.

"You all right?"

She nodded, her eyes huge pools of brilliant blue. "Just tipsy."

I steered her toward the kitchen. "Sit right here." I helped her onto a stool at the breakfast bar and fired up my coffee maker.

Moments later, I handed her a white porcelain mug of steaming coffee. "A few sips of this, you'll be good as new."

"Will you show me around?" she asked.

"Yes. If you drink your coffee."

"So bossy," she murmured. "I thought that was

Gavin's role."

Her remark made me smirk, but she took a long pull from the mug. Then she rose to her feet, happy to follow me through my apartment like a little child, eager for answers.

She stopped in front of a photo in the hall. "Is that you and Barbara Walters?"

"She's from Brookline, and we used to watch *20/20* as kids."

"Did she cover kid-friendly stories?"

"Definitely not, but our life wasn't kid-friendly to begin with."

She moved down the hall to another photo of Gavin, me, and Marchand, the Bruins' left wing. "You two look so alike and so different."

I knew what she meant. We shared a lot of similar features, but where I was usually content or smiling, Gavin was reserved and icy. Even in the pictures hanging on my walls, that much was evident. Gavin rarely smiled for a photo.

I steered Emma toward my bedroom, which was usually the last stop on the tour.

"Do you and Gavin hang out a lot?"

She was so cute and so obvious, I had to laugh, even though I hoped she'd forget about Gavin for a minute and focus on what was right in front of her. I didn't get her attraction to him, but the fact remained that if she wanted him, I wouldn't stand in the way.

"You could say that."

"Books!" she shouted, cutting me off and running to the tall cases that held dozens of books. She rubbed her index finger across the spines. Almost all my books were classics, leather-bound with gold-embossed titles.

"You're a hilarious drunk."

Emma shot me a restrained smirk. "I could see why there's no point in you going to college, you read it all anyway. Did Gavin go to college?"

I removed my suit coat and hung it in the closet, unable to answer another Gavin question for a moment. She abandoned the books and came over to sit on my bed, demanding an answer.

"Nope. Neither did Quinn." I removed my cuff links, setting them on the wooden tray on the dresser, and began to unbutton my dress shirt.

She scooted back toward the tufted headboard, her little feet reaching only the middle of the king-sized bed.

"This is so cozy. I would die for a bed like this." When she rolled face-first into a pillow and inhaled, I resisted the urge to chuckle at her again.

I pulled my dress shirt off to reveal a tight plain white tee. I savored watching Emma's eyes watching me as I undressed. She wanted my brother . . . for now. I had to remember that if he could make himself worthy of her, I wanted that for him. But if he was determined to sink the whole fucking thing?

Well, there was no reason Emma couldn't get a look at what she was missing in the meantime.

"My phone," Emma said, and tried to rise from the bed at the pinging sound coming from the other room.

"I got it, princess. Is it in your purse?" I finished removing my belt and rolled it, then placed it in the belt drawer.

"Yes, thank you." She settled back into the pillows and curled into a ball.

When I handed her the bag, she fished out her phone.

"It's Gavin." She sounded unsure and stared down at the phone for a few seconds. "I'm not going to text him back," she announced triumphantly, clearly satisfied with herself.

"And why not?" *Because you're here with me, happy and in my bed?*

"I think he probably had the wrong number." Emma drew her brows together and tossed the phone down beside her.

"Why, what did it say?" This was intriguing, and pissed me off because it was late and he couldn't possibly have a need for her now. Moreover, he knew she was out with me tonight.

Emma stared at her phone. "It says, where's my toy? So, he must have meant it for someone else who lost something."

Did Emma believe that bullshit? Since she clearly

didn't know Gavin at all, perhaps I should clue her in. "You're the toy, Emma. He expects you to fall all over him. He's a dick like that."

I watched Emma's expression fall as I spoke, wishing I could take it back instantly. *Fuck. Why did I say all that?* What the hell was the matter with me? I'd decided from the start that Emma would be perfect for Gavin, if only he would open up to the experience. But, damn it, if he couldn't live up to the task? Maybe it was time to start looking out for a guy who could.

Namely, me.

She let out a soft *oh*. That information seemed to deflate her.

I sat down on the bed next to her, moving in closer. "I'm sorry. I shouldn't have said that." I placed my hands on her shoulders, rubbing lightly.

She shook her head. "No, it's okay. I'm glad you told me the truth."

"Need anything else, princess?" I asked as I reluctantly removed my hands from her delicate shoulders.

"I'm all right." She looked again at her phone as if she was hoping for another message.

"You like Gavin," I said and held my breath, begging silently for her to convince me otherwise.

"He's arrogant and controlling," she blurted before pausing to take a deep breath. "I'm sorry. I didn't mean to say that. He's my boss, and frankly, I'm grateful for the extra money and what he's done for the library."

I pressed my lips together and waited as Emma paused.

"I guess you're my boss too, but you're so easy to be around. I can really be myself."

"Well, you're off the clock now and with a friend," I said.

"Thanks for taking care of me."

"Still cold?" I asked as I wrapped an arm around her .

She sank against me in response, resting her cheek on my chest and snuggling in. "I'm glad you brought me here."

"I couldn't have you going home and getting sick

alone. I felt bad for letting you drink so much."

She raised her head from its resting spot. "I'm not sick."

"I'm glad to hear that. Do you want me to take you home now?"

She shook her head. "I'm not ready to go just yet. Is that okay?"

"Of course."

"Do you have a bathroom I can use?"

We rose from the bed and I led her toward the master bathroom.

"Oh my word!" She gasped. "Cooper, you're in trouble. You've been holding out on me."

Emma's voice echoed around the walls. Her eyes widened as she took in the glass two-person shower, spa tub, and double vanity. My bathroom was over-the-top, and I made no apologies for that. It was complete with its own chandelier and an overstuffed armchair.

Emma climbed into the empty bathtub, fully clothed. "This is incredible."

"Can I run you a bath?" I chuckled at her.

"Really?"

"Why not? So long as you're not feeling too buzzed still?"

"Oh yes, please," she replied eagerly. "I feel a lot better. Wow, what a treat."

"You crack me up." I leaned down to lift her small body from the bath. "Mint or lavender?"

"Lavender, please."

After filling the tub and adding the apothecary scents, I brought her a long white tee shirt and a pair of boxers. "Towels are in there." I pointed to the glass cabinet in the corner, trying not to die of a throbbing hard-on at the thought of Emma Bell in my fucking bathtub. "I'll be in the living room if you need me, princess."

As I closed the door, I had to laugh.

Karma was a bitch.

Chapter Eighteen

Emma

The bath was glorious. The smell of lavender filled the room and I closed my eyes, sinking further into the hot water. The alcohol buzzing through my system had finally worn off, but my confusion over Gavin hadn't. He was in the room yesterday when Cooper asked me to attend the event tonight, so he knew I'd be with Cooper. I wanted to let myself imagine that Gavin was staking his claim on me, and at the same time, that thought disgusted me.

But I was also disgusted with myself. What the hell was I doing in Cooper's bathtub? At first, a little tipsy and seeing the glorious room, it had been totally innocent. But now, as the effects of the vodka faded, if felt anything but.

Was I subconsciously making my decision? An irreversible one, at that?

Cooper's knock echoed through the bathroom. "Emma?"

"Yes?"

Cooper opened the door and let himself in. I looked down, realizing all the bubbles had vanished. Nothing but pink skin as far as the eye could see. I folded my arms over my chest.

He held back a grin and looked away, clearing his throat. "Sorry, you, uh . . . got a phone call, and I saw who it was so I answered."

"Who was it?"

"Gavin. I told him you were in the bath." Cooper's face didn't betray his satisfaction, but his voice did.

My heart banged in my chest at his words as I considered the implication and impression they caused. Cooper watched me, waiting for my reaction.

"That's perfect, thank you." It wasn't a lie. And if Gavin felt jealous, it served him right. I didn't want to play his silly games. I was out with a sweet guy and having a damn fine time.

Cooper gave me a wide smile, seeming very pleased at my dismissal of Gavin.

"Did you need something else?" I asked as I rubbed my feet together in the warm water.

"Do you like being here with me, princess?"

I hesitated, not wanting to lead him on, but not wanting to lie either. "Yes."

He moved into the bathroom, leaving the barrier of the door behind. Leaning down, he gently kissed my forehead.

"You are so fucking perfect, it hurts," he whispered near my ear.

I didn't know what to say, so I remained frozen beneath the water. He was so sweet. So gentle. Nothing at all like Gavin. And, damn it, it felt so good to be cherished.

"Let me wash your hair. Nothing else, I swear it."

I nodded in response, my throat suddenly tight and dry. He pumped a few drops of shampoo into his hand and knelt on the floor by the tub, gentling massaging my head with his fingers.

"Mmm . . . that feels good." I leaned back into his big hands. No one ever pampered me like this, and even though doubt lingered in the back of my mind, I wanted to enjoy the moment.

An excess of lather built and suds slid down my neck and chest. Cooper's breathing quickened, but his touch was controlled. He worked his way from my scalp to the ends of my hair, until he was massaging my neck and shoulders with the thick white foam. After he rinsed my hair, he conditioned it, taking his time stroking my locks until all the tangles were gone.

I glanced at Cooper's intense stare and felt my cheeks burn, so I looked away and flicked the drain open with my toe. He opened a huge towel and lifted me when I stood, wrapping me inside and carrying me back to his bed. He sat me down and grabbed the clothes he'd brought for me. Cooper turned to face the wall, and I let the towel drop and slipped the sweatshirt on as guilty feelings began to stir.

How bad was it to come on Gavin's fingers one day and then get naked in Cooper's tub the next? Super bad or just a little bad? I couldn't face him, feeling more confused than ever. My chances with Gavin might have just slipped away with that bath water, but maybe that was a good thing.

"I-I think I better get going." I looked down at my

lap, my head spinning, and wondered if maybe I was still tipsier than I thought.

"I'll call you a car, princess."

When Cooper left the room, I slipped on the huge sweatpants he'd brought for me, cinching the waist tight to keep them from falling. I gathered my dress and purse and headed down the hall, finding my shoes by the door. High heels and sweatpants? No, no one would think this was a walk of shame. Bare feet in the city was not an option, however, so I slipped on the heels as Cooper came over, laughing at the sight.

"You like my new look?" I turned around for him, and he nodded.

"Car's out front. I'll walk you out." Cooper held my hand as we entered the elevator, and when the doors opened in the lobby, he peeked around. "Coast is clear."

I smiled at him. "I look good in heels and sweats."

After planting an innocent kiss on his scruffy cheek, I stepped into the car and pulled out my phone, looking back at the call log to see how long the brothers had spoken. About five minutes. Were they talking about me the whole time? What did Gavin say was the reason for calling me? I should have asked Cooper, but I knew it would offend him to talk more about Gavin. He was patient all night with my many questions.

I opened my messages and wrote to Gavin, *I'm sorry*. I read the words over and over and debated sending. Deciding against it, I pushed to delete the text and accidentally sent it. Damn this new phone.

The phone pinged almost instantly, and Gavin's text read, *Why, did something happen with Cooper?*

My heart rose into my throat, and I debated lying before texting back a simple, *Yes*. He replied a few minutes later as the car pulled up to my building, *Why would I care?*

I wrote back quickly, *Why else would you have asked?*

Damn, Gavin could be such a child. Cooper would never play a game like this; he'd just tell me he wanted me. Maybe Gavin was a bit more damaged. He had textbook anger issues, after all.

Reading his final response, *Glad you had fun with my brother*, I almost threw my phone down on the seat.

"Thanks," I called to the driver, my irritation obvious. Fucking Gavin. It was his idea in the first place that I should work with both of them.

My house looked drab in comparison to Cooper's high-end palace. I threw my purse and keys on the kitchen table and poured myself a tall water. The sounds of my neighbor's TV bled through the walls, and a siren wailed outside. Cooper's apartment had been quiet save for the light music that played through a built-in speaker system.

I flopped on my bed and curled up in the blankets. It was getting late, but there was no chance I could sleep. I felt a deep sense of shame about Cooper and the bathtub.

I typed out and erased a dozen messages to Gavin, some apologetic, some admitting that I'd stalked him for nearly a year, some telling him off.

And what about Cooper? Did I owe him an apology too? I hated the thought of leading him on.

When did my life get so confusing?

Chapter Nineteen

Cooper

Ever since I'd answered Emma's phone, Gavin had been acting like a complete cockhead, snapping at me, Quinn, Sonja, and anyone else in his path. But through it all, he still hadn't asked me the question. The one I knew was burning a hole in his gut.

Now, the two of us sat alone in Quinn's office, the smell of food lingering in the air between us along with the tension. As we waited for Quinn, I wondered if Gavin would finally break.

"Where the fuck is he?" Gavin barked.

"Chill out. He'll be here."

"Don't tell me to chill. Ever. I'm starting without him." Gavin grabbed a container of noodles and filled his plate.

"I'm here, boys. Now play nice," Quinn said as he came in and shut the door. I filled my own plate as he slid into the seat across from Gavin. "What's your problem today?" Quinn asked him.

"Cooper's smug," Gavin said before helping himself to a forkful of pad thai.

"No, I asked what your problem was. Cooper being smug is Cooper's problem," Quinn said.

"I don't have a problem then."

"So, this is about Emma," Quinn said.

"Yes," I answered as Gavin gave a resounding, "No."

When Quinn and I said "liar" in unison, a deeper scowl formed on Gavin's face. He looked down at his plate, digging in once again.

"Gavin's been flying solo a long time," Quinn said. "Seems to me he really likes Emma and doesn't want to admit it to us."

At that, Gavin rolled his eyes, then glared at me. "What happened with Emma last weekend?"

Quinn and I looked at each other, both in shock at the very revealing question. Gavin did like her. More than he was letting on.

Shit.

It was what I wanted. Or, part of me did, at least. But

I couldn't deny I was getting attached to little Emma Bell myself.

"We went out, I brought her back to my place, she got undressed and enjoyed my spa tub . . ."

Gavin was hanging on my every word as Quinn shot me a stern look of warning.

Suddenly, Gavin let out a muttered snarl and pushed his unfinished plate across the table, then stood and left the room.

Quinn shook his head at me. "Why'd you have to do that, Coop? You know he has a harder time with this stuff than you. You win women over all the time, and you know he's been alone for a long time now. Maybe this is the one for him."

I hated when Quinn was right. And, damn it, I knew Emma wanted Gavin too, even though he wasn't treating her the way she deserved.

But I loved my brother. At the end of the day, what I wanted most was to see him happy.

I released a heavy sigh and stood to follow Gavin, who'd retreated to his office. Alyssa eyed me as I passed her desk and knocked on his door.

"Go the fuck away, please," Gavin called back.

I opened the door and closed us inside his office. "Do you like her or not? Tell me now, last chance."

"Nope. She's all yours. You've already had her, anyway."

"So if I didn't have her already, do you like her?" I demanded, clenching my fists at my sides. If only he knew what this was costing me, maybe he'd show one ounce of appreciation.

"No." Gavin looked into my eyes without blinking.

"All right, then."

Gavin creased his brow at me. "But I like how she handles herself as an escort, so I may still take her out sometime."

Liar. As if we didn't have a host of professionals who would suit him just fine.

If I didn't know it before, I was starting to understand that Gavin was even more damaged that I'd ever assumed. After growing up without a mother's love, all I desired was love, intimacy, and affection at the end of a long day.

But Gavin craved control—plain and simple. Because if he was calling the shots, he could never get hurt.

We were totally different, but there was no question we were headed for a collision course—and soon—when it came to Emma Bell.

And something told me that one of us was going to find ourselves in a world of pain.

Chapter Twenty

Gavin

It had been five days since I'd last seen Emma, and every second seemed to tick on for an eternity.

In all the time we'd been apart, I'd tried to focus on my work, tried to look for new marketing opportunities and ensure the girls and clients were happy. But I couldn't.

Instead, I spent my time brainstorming lists of all the reasons these five days were a good thing, a cleansing experience. There was no doubt I was getting in over my head, and if I sank any deeper, I knew where it would lead—to the one place I wouldn't, couldn't go.

But knowing that didn't make life any easier.

I would close my eyes at night and see her sapphire gaze looking back at me in my dreams. I would climb into the shower, then imagine her ... writhing beneath my touch.

Damn, I was losing it.

Gritting my teeth, I closed out the document I'd

been working on and pinched the bridge of my nose.

If Cooper wanted her so bad, then why had he practically wheedled me into agreeing to see Emma in the first place? No, if anyone deserved to be with her, even if it was only for a brief while, it was me.

It was my fingers she'd ridden to the brink of ecstasy in the back of my limo. My name on her lips when she'd begged for more.

It wasn't just that I wanted to see her. It was that my palms itched whenever I merely thought about touching her smooth skin. My heart pounded when I thought about her smile. I breathed deeply just thinking about that light, sweet scent on the air around her. It was a craving that needed to be satisfied.

And there was only one way I'd be able to fulfill the need.

"Fuck it." I shoved out of my desk chair and pulled my phone from my pocket. Shooting off a few quick texts, I prepared myself for the date I'd always wanted with Emma—no business, no awkward small talk. Just the two of us, someplace private.

When the arrangements were in place, I took a deep breath and dialed her number. The phone only rang twice before she picked up.

"Gavin," she said, slightly breathless.

"What are you doing today?"

The long pause on the other end of the line told me she was more than a little surprised I was calling.

Welcome to the club.

"I was going to do a little more work on my house today."

"Can you hold off for another day?"

"I . . ." She hummed and then cleared her throat. "I might be able to—"

"Good. I'll be at your place in forty minutes."

I hung up, and already, I could feel my pulse throbbing in my neck and my wrists, just at the thought of seeing Emma again. I quickly I made my way to my limo, instructing Ben about our plans for the day before speeding off on our first errand.

By the time I got to Emma's place, I was still ten

minutes early, but I didn't care. I walked up her newly repaired stoop, noticing the new planters at the sides of the top step, then rapped on the door with quick, decisive knocks.

It only took a second for the door to open, and I forced myself to swallow hard.

Emma was stunning. Not just in the way she always was, but in a way that was simpler, more herself, no gown or high heels in sight. She had left her hair loose and wavy around her shoulders, and was wearing a casual off-the-shoulder top paired with cut-off jean shorts so enticing, I had to force myself not to stare at those curvy hips.

"Am I dressed okay?" she asked. "I wasn't really sure what to—"

I held up a hand to stop her. "You look perfect. Now, come on. We have people waiting on us."

"We do?" She furrowed her brow, but only paused for a moment before locking the door behind her and following me down the steps to the car. "Where are we going?"

"It's a surprise. But hopefully a good one."

I opened the door for her and she slid inside, giving me a peek of that heart-shaped ass as she ducked into the car. Quickly, I slid after her and closed the door behind us before Ben pulled out into traffic.

"Where are we going?" Emma asked once we were settled.

"You're going to love it." I grinned, though I didn't reveal anything else until Ben finally arrived at the helipad.

"A helicopter?"

I barely caught her words as we stepped from the car onto the wide space, the air around us gusty. The whirring blades left no question about why they called it a chopper.

"It's loud!" Emma said, keeping pace beside me.

I nodded. "You okay?"

"Better than okay. This is amazing."

Carefully, I placed my hand on her lower back and guided her inside, showing her how to put on her headphones and talk into her microphone.

The pilot smiled at us and gave us a thumbs-up, which Emma returned with a grin before screaming into her microphone.

"What on earth made you think of a helicopter?"

"It's a great way to travel." I returned her grin as we lifted into the air and began our journey. The whole way, Emma gripped my hand, almost like she was afraid she might fall out of the helicopter without my support, and I gave her a reassuring squeeze.

"Where are we going?" she asked again.

I shook my head. "You'll see soon enough."

The city skyline became nothing by glittery peaks and gray valleys as we ascended, and Emma stared down in amazement, pointing at the tiny skyscrapers with her mouth agape.

"This is incredible."

"It is nice, isn't it? It's even better from the front."

"You can fly one of these things?" Wide-eyed, she stared at me, and I nodded again.

"It's a passion of mine," I admitted, again revealing more of myself without even realizing it until it was done.

How did she manage that? To draw me out of the titanium shell I'd built around myself so easily?

"You should have piloted. I'd love to see you fly," she replied with a grin.

"Maybe next time."

Damn it. Not a promise, per se. But with every moment we spent together, I was digging in deeper. Committing more. Protecting myself less.

All it took was one squeeze from her soft little hand to send that thought skittering away again.

I was happier than I'd been in days. Years, maybe. No fucking way I was going to let myself ruin it.

We soared over the city, then past the rocky coastline of Massachusetts, taking the scenic route as I'd instructed our pilot. Finally, we came to rest on the helipad my favorite winery had added last year at my request.

I thanked the pilot with a nod and helped Emma from the helicopter. Then I guided her away again as the wind whipped our faces and the pilot ascended, leaving us alone at last.

When the helicopter was a speck in the air, the buzz of the blades was replaced by the gentle hum of bugs and birds in the woods beyond. I took Emma by the hand, leading her toward the entrance of the winery, and the owner came out to greet me per usual.

"Mr. Kingsley, we haven't seen you in ages."

"Hey, Edgar, great to see you again. You have our room ready, I trust."

"Absolutely, Mr. Kingsley. Absolutely."

Edgar's gaze wandered to Emma, and if I didn't know he was happily married—to a man—I might have slugged him.

"Edgar, I'd like you to meet Emma."

"It's a pleasure to meet you, dear." Edgar extended his hand to Emma.

"You too, Edgar. Really nice to meet you."

"Your cart is ready." Edgar motioned toward the golf cart that sat a short distance away on a gravel path.

I hopped in the driver seat and Emma slid in next to me, and we took off down the path toward the private tasting room I'd reserved for the day. Admittedly, Edgar wasn't happy with me when I told him to move the small wedding party he had scheduled because I'd like to bring a date here today, but he made it happen.

"This is stunning, Gavin. It's so peaceful here." Emma's voice was in awe as we drove through the picturesque pathway to the vineyards. Huge old oak trees and towering pines were set against rolling hills, and ahead, acres and acres of grapevines twined around trellis posts.

"Here's our stop. I hope you're hungry." I pointed ahead to an intimate tasting room. The small stone building was covered in Boston ivy and smelled powerfully from the rows of clay pots filled with every herb imaginable.

"Mr. Kingsley!" Cecily, the sommelier, waved vigorously at us as we pulled up.

"Do you ever get tired of that greeting?" Emma asked me.

I shook my head and took her hand, leading her inside the tasting room. Cecily beckoned us forward.

"Good afternoon. We've paired a few of your favorite wines with some local seasonal treats selected by our chef. Please enjoy. I'll be around in the vineyard if you should need me." And with that, she was gone, stepping out the French doors of the private cottage and closing them behind her.

The winery had pulled out all the stops. Mountains of cheeses, mounds of figs, crystal bowls filled with amber honey, pillows of spiced butters, and an array of homemade breadsticks covered the elegant table alongside a selection of my favorite wines—red, white, and even rosé. Each was labeled with a suggested food pairing, and Emma ran her fingers over the elegant tabletop as she read each tiny sign.

"You arranged for all of this?" she asked softly. "How did you even know about this place?"

"When you go to as many events as I do, you end up trying a lot of wine. This is my favorite. I called and asked them to set up a special date for us today."

She shook her head. "All this . . . it's incredible."

"I'm glad you like it. Let's dig in."

Emma didn't need to be told twice. Picking up one of the earthenware plates from a corner of the table, she loaded her plate with stuffed figs, fresh grapes, goat cheese, and olive-oil breadsticks before pouring herself a small measure of red wine.

We took our plates to the small seating area that overlooked a large picture window, sinking down into plush leather armchairs, our plates balanced on our knees.

"It looks like you've gotten a good amount of work done on your grandmother's place," I said.

She beamed. "Did you notice? It's been incredible. All the moldings are fixed, and I found an old rocker just like she used to have by the bay window. It's really coming along."

"Who did you hire?" I asked, taking a sip of red wine.

She blinked. "Hire?"

"To do the work for you?"

"Nobody." She took a bite of her fig and cheese. "I watched some very informative YouTube videos, though."

"You did all that yourself?"

Emma nodded, and I found myself yet again amazed by her.

"Impressive."

"I like to think so." She grinned. "I may have to get a contractor for my kitchen counters soon, though."

"Or you could entrust things to a team of brothers you know," I offered. "We're pretty handy."

She grimaced. "I don't know about all that. You and Cooper together, in my house . . . all that testosterone and masculine energy. I'm not sure I could handle that."

Chapter Twenty-One

Emma

As I watched Gavin take another sip of chilled pinot grigio, a sense of euphoria washed over me. I had no idea he had it in him to plan something so extravagant.

And against all odds, I was falling for this man, for his dominant personality, sexy attitude, and even sexier physique. He was a high-maintenance man, unlike anyone I'd ever been around before. At times, he was such a hard-ass, so demanding and intense. Other times, it was like he was my own personal Prince Charming, taking me away on a helicopter, making sure I'd eaten, and telling me I was beautiful. It was all so dizzying.

This certainly felt like more than we'd agreed to. I was supposed to accompany him to business dinners and charity events, not be whisked away for romantic afternoons at his favorite vineyard.

"Forgive me. I wasn't thinking," he said.

"What?"

"You don't really drink and I've brought you to a

vineyard. It's not my smoothest moment."

Smiling, I leaned close and pressed a soft kiss to his mouth. "Are you kidding? I love it here."

And I loved this side of Gavin even more. He was being so real and vulnerable, sharing a piece of himself with me.

Despite my heart's warning, despite the alarm bells ringing in my head, I was developing real feelings for this man. Briefly, I wondered if I should end this—demand that he and his brother release me from this strange arrangement, and go off on my own to collect myself before I made a horrendous mistake. But the other half of me knew it was already too late. I was Gavin's, like it or not.

Yet there was something I needed to get off my chest, something that had been weighing on my mind all morning. Turning toward Gavin, I gathered my thoughts.

"What is it?" he asked, ever intuitive as he stroked his thumb over the line creasing my forehead.

"I've given it some thought, and I don't feel right about this arrangement anymore."

This time, Gavin's brows drew together. "You don't enjoy your time with me?"

I shook my head. "It's not that. I just . . . this feels more like a date, not work. I would be here with you just because you asked, even if it weren't for the money, and I don't feel right keeping it."

His posture relaxed. "Fine. And for the record, this is a date, Emma."

"Oh." Now I felt stupid for not knowing the difference. Of course this was a date. He'd arranged for a private helicopter ride and wine tasting. But I was glad he knew where I stood.

Gavin leaned down and pressed a soft kiss to my lips. "And what about Cooper?" he asked, moving a lock of hair behind my shoulder.

"What about him?"

Gavin shrugged. "Just trying to understand where this all stands."

Taking a deep breath, I shifted closer to Gavin, enjoying this softer side of him. Did this mean he wanted me all to himself? "Cooper and I are friends. You and I are . . . more, I hope."

"More." The word rolled off his tongue so quickly, I couldn't tell if he meant it as a question or as a statement.

"I think my days as an escort are behind me," I said.

"Fair enough. But if I should need a date for an event?" he asked, his tone playful.

"Then I guess you'll have to ask me and see." Our conversation had me feeling mischievous, like I'd won some power back in this exchange.

"So, you and Cooper never . . ."

I shook my head. "No."

"Even when he lured you to his place and got you naked in his tub?" Gavin raised one dark brow at me.

Cooper had hardly lured me. I'd been so confused back then, so desperate for attention as I ping-ponged between these two men. The truth was I'd drank too much and had made a fool of myself.

Stalling, I took a sip of my wine. "He washed my hair. That was all."

Gavin seemed pleased by my response, drawing my chin up and bringing his mouth to mine. "My fingers are the only ones that have been inside you?"

I nodded.

"That makes me very happy, Emma."

Gavin set his wineglass on the little cocktail table that separated us, and did the same with mine. Leaning close, he brought his mouth to my neck.

"What about the staff? Won't Cecily be back to check on us?" I asked.

"Hmm. Don't care," he murmured against my throat. "Want you."

He peppered my neck in soft kisses while his large palms roamed over my bare legs. While we kissed, he drew me up so we were both standing. I brought my arms around him, my breasts aching at the contact of his firm chest.

Finally, his mouth captured mine in an urgent kiss. It was electric. Raw. Molten. His tongue moved expertly against mine, sending my blood spiraling through my veins.

Sliding his hand along the hem of my shorts, Gavin's deft fingers made contact with my panties, sending a spark of electricity skittering through my veins. "Hang on tight. This is going to be fast."

I didn't know what he meant at first until he breached my underwear and pushed two fingers inside me, making my breath catch.

"Gavin . . ." I whimpered, holding on for dear life.

He kissed me again, seemingly oblivious to my intense pleasure. Even his fingers were big—I couldn't imagine what the rest of him might be like.

As he sent me racing toward climax within minutes, I clutched Gavin's shoulders for support, rocking my hips into his hand and kissing him like my very life depended on it. Working myself against him, I felt the huge ridge in his pants pressing insistently into my hip, the only thing that signaled his excitement.

I came undone quickly and without warning.

"Gavin!" I cried out, my body quaking around his fingers.

"That's it. So beautiful." He pulled back a fraction to

watch me.

Rather than feel self-conscious like the old me would have done, I reveled in his attention, dropping my head back and squeezing my eyes closed as the most intense orgasm I'd ever had washed over me.

When it was through, Gavin withdrew his hand and licked his fingers clean, and my vaginal muscles clenched again at the lust-filled look in his eyes.

"So perfect," he murmured.

Before I had time to wonder if he was going to let me touch him this time, Gavin growled, "Take out my cock."

Pulling back an inch so I could see his eyes, I felt confusion washed over me. "What do you want?"

"What do *you* want, Emma?"

My gaze wandered toward the wall of windows that were only feet away, and though Gavin seemed to have no issues with public displays as I recalled from the limo, I also knew somehow that he'd want our first time to be more private.

"Well, I don't think you're going to fuck me . . ."

"You're correct about that."

My hand gripped his firm erection. It felt huge and insistent. "Then I'd like to please you with my mouth." The words surprised me. It seemed Gavin was turning me into a sexual creature with each passing day we spent together.

"That would make me very happy."

I slid to the floor in front of him, balancing on my knees, ignoring the way the wooden floor bit into my skin. Lowering the zipper to his pants, I found him already hard and nearly bursting through the fabric of his black boxer briefs. I ran my palm against him, appreciating his size.

Gavin looked down, smirking at me. "You don't have to be so delicate with me."

Okay, then. When I tugged his pants and boxers down his hips, his cock sprang free and bobbed enticingly in front of me.

He was massive—a thick shaft and a wide tip, and well-groomed to complete the most perfect package I had ever seen.

Testing him, I bought my mouth forward and swirled my tongue across the blunt tip of him.

A small grunt of approval in the back of his throat urged me deeper.

Gripping the last several inches I couldn't fit into my mouth, I stroked him firmly.

"Take all of it."

Pulling back, I met his eyes. "I can't, sir."

"I know that. But watching you try is precious, pet." He stroked my hair, taking himself in hand and bringing his wide tip to my lips.

I opened, obeying his command, and Gavin slid several inches deeper. Breathing through my nose, I battled with myself to accept him.

Finally, he slid deeper, rewarding me with a soft groan. "Fuck."

I pushed forward, urged on by his cries of pleasure, and for several minutes, I pleasured him with my mouth, loving the masculine sounds he made, until finally, a hot jet of semen streamed down my throat.

"Jesus, pet." He raked his fingers through my hair, looking down at me with adoration.

Pulling me to my feet, Gavin continued caressing me while my heart pounded heavily in my chest.

Chapter Twenty-Two

Gavin

Leaning down, I pressed a kiss to Emma's forehead. "Are you okay?"

She nodded.

"Not too chilly?"

Pulling her into my lap once again, I ran my hands along her bare arms, wondering if her chill bumps were the result of the air-conditioning or something else. Did she feel this connection buzzing between us as strongly as I did?

"I'm good."

When I lifted Emma's chin so she would meet my eyes, her hazy gaze almost undid me. Glassy-eyed and flushed, her lips swollen and pink from pleasuring me, she was perfect. Watching her swallow me down was more erotic than anything, *ever*. And I'd done some kinky shit.

In that moment, I was hit with a flurry of emotions. Elation? Yes. Pleasure? Hell yeah. But it was more than that. I was totally and utterly losing it, and our erotic encounter had me questioning if I was falling apart, or finally coming together.

"I like you like this," I murmured, petting her cheek with my thumb.

"Like what?"

Several words flashed through my mind at once. *Docile. Soft. Mine.* "Submissive," I settled on.

Emma pursed her lips as though tasting the word. "I didn't know I was."

"With me you are."

She couldn't argue.

Inhaling a deep breath against the rush of sudden and unexpected emotion, I took her hand. The way she placed her hand in mine was so natural, so effortless. And her small palm fit perfectly inside my much larger hand.

"Should we go?"

"Home?" The hint of disappointment in her voice was unmistakable.

"No. I have somewhere else in mind." I was

changing my plans for her. This might take me down a dangerous path, but fuck it. I was too far in to walk away now. "Are you hungry?"

For more than cock this time, my naughty brain supplied. I brushed my thumb against her full lower lip again, unable to stop myself.

Her expression was guarded, but happy. "I could eat."

Whisking her away today had been impulsive, the need to see her welling up inside me until it couldn't be refused any longer, as was my suggestion we continue our date with dinner. Apparently, Emma brought out a spontaneous side to me I didn't know I had.

"Let's get out of here." I ushered her into the cart and drove her toward the grassy hill on the vineyard where the chopper would be waiting to take us wherever I asked. I was thinking about the casual neighborhood pizzeria I hadn't been to in forever. "Do you like pizza?"

Her answering smile told me everything I needed to know.

• • •

"Alyssa?" I gritted my teeth, forcing down the string of curse words I wanted to let rip. "A moment of your time, please?"

"Right away, Mr. Kingsley."

I'd asked her to call me Gavin about four thousand times over the past year and a half, but that never seemed to faze her. Not that I was going to complain; I appreciated the formality. Growing up the way I had, I wasn't going to criticize a show of respect.

Strolling in a second later, Alyssa stopped in front of my desk. "What did you need?"

I took a deep breath and composed myself. "These summary reports are all messed up."

She frowned. "I double-checked them. Everything should be spot-on. You're probably just not used to the new format."

"New format?" I felt my temples starting to throb.

Alyssa nodded, taking a step toward my desk. "Yes. It was Cooper's suggestion. Let me show you. It takes some getting used to."

Fucking Cooper. How many times had I uttered that phrase over the past two weeks? Good fucking question.

While Alyssa gave me a quick tutorial on the various tabs of the spreadsheet, my mind wandered back to my day at the vineyard with Emma last weekend.

Reflecting on the way I'd pushed her to her limits, I felt my heart kick up a notch. She'd given in so easily, riding my hand and murmuring soft, pleasure-filled whimpers as she got closer, and then coming apart so beautifully, despite the risk of us being discovered by the ever-attentive staff.

And then when she wanted to pleasure me? I didn't have the stomach to turn her away again. I'd let her drop to her knees on the dusty pine floor and take me. Watching her force my wide length into her mouth and cradle me in her delicate hands? Fuck. I almost got hard just remembering it.

Even better yet was her refusal to take part in the game Cooper and I had lured her into. Her strength continued to arouse me.

"That will be all, Alyssa," I barked, realizing my assistant was still standing there.

Stifling an eye roll, Alyssa turned and strolled from my office. She closed the door behind her, clearly annoyed.

But I wasn't worried about my assistant. My mind was already spinning on when I could see Emma again. My gaze drifted toward the wall of windows where little pings of rain were hitting the glass. I needed to plan another date, something different this time. Something more intimate.

It was time to make my move, time to say to hell with all my brothers' ominous warnings and take what was mine.

Chapter Twenty-Three

Gavin

Friday evening, I picked up Emma from her neat little brownstone.

"No driver tonight," she murmured, climbing in beside me.

I reached out toward her, gripping her hand in mine. "I wanted you all alone. I'm selfish like that."

The smile she treated me to was warm and dazzling. "Are we on our way to the restaurant?" she asked at the rapidly changing scenery. We'd entered a seedier part of town, someplace I doubted she'd ever seen. For her sake, I hoped she'd never been here.

I shook my head and turned down the side street that led to my destination. I still remembered this area like the back of my hand, though it had been many years since I'd visited.

"Not just yet. There's something I want to show you first."

Lately, for no reason at all, my mind would wander

to memories of my childhood, to my mother. I remembered her traipsing around the apartment in the evenings, long after I should have been asleep. She'd turn on her ancient record player, listening to John Coltrane or Miles Davis. The music was so bluesy and sad, but with a hidden depth. It fit my mother perfectly. Beautiful and tragic, all at the same time.

I recalled the way she'd lean over the side of the lumpy twin mattress I shared with Cooper and press a soft kiss to my forehead. She wore a white satin robe, tied loosely at the waist. I remembered catching a glimpse of the white satin panties she wore, and the peek of a cherry-tipped breast, and while I was still too young to understand, I knew enough to know I shouldn't look but wanted to all the same. It was simple curiosity. I knew the parts my brothers and I had, basic utilitarian things used for pissing and nothing else. I knew enough to know my mother was different, saw the way men would stop and stare at her, and shout lewd things to her on the street. She must have had something special under that robe, but what, I didn't know.

We repeated the same scenario night after night. After dinner, she'd drink a glass of something so strong, the scent of it on her breath made my eyes sting when she kissed my head. She'd dress in a white jean miniskirt or a pair of cut-off jean shorts and a halter top, then fix her makeup and hair. Then she'd tell Quinn to lock the door and not answer it for anyone.

I remembered the hot tears that stung my eyes when I begged her to stay, which I inevitably did night after night. She'd ruffle my hair and chuckle at me, not even giving me a backward glance as she lifted the arm on her record player, silencing it before strolling out the apartment door.

I didn't understand what she did for a living, and had fought with the boys at school who told me my mom spread her legs for money. It wasn't until I was thirteen that Quinn confirmed the truth and I'd finally accepted it. I didn't talk to my mother for a week after that, until she'd finally snapped at me and told me to grow up. So, I had. And a few years later, she was gone.

Even as I drove Emma through the streets I used to wander, I found myself growing increasingly quiet. I couldn't bring myself to burst her bubble. She'd grown up so differently, probably hadn't known this life existed, which was fine by me. I didn't want to see the pity in her eyes, didn't want her to know about the struggles, the weeks we ate nothing but hot dogs because we'd run out of money, the schoolyard fights I'd gotten into when a classmate accused my mother of sleeping with his father.

Maybe it was stupid to come here, but reflecting on the fact that I'd pushed her so hard on our date and she'd given in so beautifully, I'd wanted to do something different this time, something to let her into my world just a tiny bit more.

I stopped beside an alley that was filled with garbage, broken-down furniture, and an overflowing dumpster. It was quite a sight.

"Gavin?" she asked, her voice steady but filled with questions.

"I know you think you know me and you've got me figured out, but it wasn't always like this. I told you that I came from nothing."

Emma nodded, her eyes widening as she took in our surroundings again. "Where are we?"

My very humble beginning was splayed out for her to see, and instead of making me feel bare and exposed, I simply felt numb.

I pointed up ahead to a decaying seven-story red brick building. "We grew up right there. Third floor, middle unit."

All three of us boys and my mother had shared a two-bedroom, one-bathroom apartment. We'd lived that way until I was seventeen. Only when my mother passed away did we finally leave the projects and the government-subsidized housing we'd grown up in. Seeing it all again felt surreal, and suddenly I doubted my decision to bring Emma here.

Christ, this is depressing.

I pointed up ahead to the next block. "We walked to the school two blocks down. I used to hang out on that street corner with a pack of hoodlums who are all probably either dead or in jail today."

Why in God's name we'd stayed here all those years, I had no clue. During the good years, my mother had enough funds to move us away, yet we'd stayed. Then the money slowed—or rather, my mother got older and her clients became fewer and further between—and we were stuck.

When Quinn hit sixteen, he'd gotten a job doing manual labor at a nearby construction site, and I'd started bagging groceries at the local supermarket. We'd shielded Cooper the best we could, funneling him lunch money or his favorite gummy bears when we could. Even at age fourteen, I'd had my priorities straight. The rent payment came first, groceries next, the electric bill and so on. New clothes and shoes weren't even on our radar. Now, of course, I tended to overindulge and spoil myself. Growing up without, I definitely enjoyed the finer things.

Gazing off into the distance, I could still remember my mother strolling down the street in her chic wool coat with its fuzzy faux-fur collar tucked up under her chin, tramping through the snow in her high-heeled boots. She'd loved this dilapidated little neighborhood. She knew every shopkeeper, every neighbor, and made sure they all looked out for us.

She was a single mother of three boys doing her best. She never spoke of my father, and the few times I'd tried to ask about him, she'd barked, *He's not here now, is he? So, forget about him.*

My mother pushed hard work and education above

all else. She hadn't graduated from high school, but demanded our attendance and good grades. I knew it was her unconventional example of work ethic that pushed me today.

Emma watched a drunk stumble past our car, cursing loudly and waving his fist. She turned toward me, concern in her eyes. "I don't know what to say. Why are you letting me in like this?"

Looking straight ahead, I took in one last glance at the place that had been my home for so many years. I'd heard the city planned to tear this building down in a few months. It was filled with lead paint and asbestos, and the housing authority had deemed it unfit.

I shrugged. "Just felt like reminiscing, I guess."

It might not have been the most romantic gesture, but it was all I had. Emma could have said no that first day in my office, but instead she'd agreed to our arrangement. This was my way of reciprocating and letting her in too.

Emma's eyes widened as she took in our surroundings. Not missing a single detail, she gazed out on the street. "Thank you for showing me."

"Ready to get out of here?"

She nodded.

I drove us toward the highway, punching the accelerator harder than necessary, eager to leave this part of the city in the past where it belonged.

When we pulled up to the French restaurant I'd chosen for dinner, I parked right in front.

Emma peered out the window. "Are you sure it's open?"

I nodded. "I rented the restaurant for the evening. The chef is a friend of mine. A client, actually."

Emma's eyes widened and her mouth lifted into a smile. "So, it'll be just us?"

"Indeed."

Once inside the dim restaurant, I led Emma back to the table near the fireplace, my favorite spot. Quite the dichotomy, from the projects to fine dining. I could tell by Emma's expression that the irony wasn't lost on either of us.

We had a simple meal of perfectly cooked steak and

green salad. I was pleased the conversation flowed easily between us, hints of that sexual chemistry I'd come to expect zapping between us as we spoke.

"Will you tell me more about your childhood?" Emma finally asked.

I'd been wondering if she would after what I'd shown her tonight.

"Another time." My mind had had enough of exploring memory lane, and my blood was burning for Emma. I left a stack of bills on the table and rose. "Let's get out of here."

Chapter Twenty-Four

Emma

Tonight, Gavin had shown me a side of himself that I was still coming to grips with. Inexplicably, he'd let me into his world—shown me a painful glimpse of his past, treating me to a front-row seat to all of it.

I knew from Cooper that they'd had a rough childhood, but I never could have imagined what our little tour entailed. Driving through those streets, seeing his run-down neighborhood and the desolate apartment building he'd called home, I still had chill bumps on my arms just thinking about it. Graffiti-littered streets and women waiting on street corners weren't a part of my upbringing. But they had been his, and he'd entrusted me with that knowledge.

To know that even now he only lived thirty minutes away from it all, it made me realize that his painful past might not be so distant after all. I knew it wasn't something he'd share with just anyone. As strange as it sounded, that was special to me, and for that reason, it was a memory I'd cherish.

It probably hadn't been the best idea to go touring the slums in a brand-new Mercedes, yet I'd never felt unsafe. With Gavin by my side, I'd felt secure in the knowledge that he could handle anything that came our way.

I would never forget his expression when he'd parked. The hard set of his jaw, the feel of his warm palm on my knee, the sleek, luxurious interior of his car where we sat safely cocooned against the stark poverty outside our windows. It was an experience I'd never expected.

But then again, with Gavin I was learning to expect the unexpected.

As close as we'd grown, I knew he was still holding a part of himself back, but I had a feeling tonight was going to change that. Maybe it was because of the way he'd made himself so vulnerable today, or because of the sweet dinner date he'd planned. But with the way his voice had gone husky and his eyes had blazed with passion when he asked if I was ready to leave—I knew he was taking me home.

My skin tingled with the desire for his hands, my body warm and flushed with the secret knowledge that tonight was going to be the night we'd have sex for the first time.

I certainly wasn't a virgin, so none of this should have felt new or nerve-racking to me, but it did—incredibly so. Gavin wouldn't be like my other lovers; I knew that for certain. And the anticipation was killing me. I wanted my hands on him, wanted to feel the weight of his body on mine.

And there would be no going back.

We drove on, turning right onto an almost-deserted street lit with pretty streetlights for another few minutes, until finally pulling into an underground parking garage. Gavin used a keycard to gain entrance, and the mechanical gate slid open silently to admit us.

After pulling into a designated spot right next to the car I recognized as his driver's, Gavin killed the engine.

"Are you ready?"

I nodded and unlatched my seat belt.

Outside the car, I swayed in my heels, the wine we'd enjoyed at dinner catching up with me. Gavin reached for my elbow, steadying me. He took my purse, holding the strap in his free hand, and led me toward the elevator.

The sight of Gavin holding my deep purple clutch—this big alpha male, well over six feet of solid muscle—it made my heart swell. He certainly knew his way into my panties, but my heart? Was that open to him too?

Before I had time to ponder that, the doors to the elevator closed and Gavin's muscular frame was pinning me to the wall, his mouth descending firmly over mine. As he nipped at my bottom lip, I knew as long as I lived, I'd never tire of his kisses. The way his tongue moved expertly against mine, the way he coaxed soft moans from my throat despite my best efforts to remain as neutral as he seemed, it was intoxicating. I was drunk on him, and still I wanted more.

The elevator doors opened to an atrium with skylights that I was sure were beautiful during the day, but tonight they were almost eerie, revealing midnight-blue sky and the soft glow of the moon up above.

Gavin stopped in front of a large pale gray door, the only one in the atrium, and entered his code until I heard the lock click.

"I'm surprised it's not the penthouse."

"That's a bunch of overpriced nonsense. I have the entire floor to myself. I do have some limits, pet." His mouth pulled into a smirk that made my belly flip.

His home was immaculate. A kitchen greeted us first, outfitted with black granite, chrome fixtures, and gray cabinetry that looked so high-end, I was afraid to touch anything. Next, we passed by a formal living room and dining room that I wondered if he ever used. Soft gray silk drapes hung from the ceiling, framing huge picture windows that overlooked an impressive cityscape.

Gavin led me deeper into his apartment, past well-appointed furniture and art. Apparently, he wasn't kidding about owning the entire fifteenth floor of the building. He stopped in a cozy den with an oversized sofa, a worn leather ottoman, and a flat-screen TV mounted to the wall above a gas fireplace. A side table was strewn with magazines like *The Economist* and *Architectural Digest*, along with his laptop.

Part of me wondered if this was where he spent his evenings—the hum of the TV in the background while he worked on his laptop until exhaustion overtook him and he wandered alone to his bedroom. Then again, why did I assume he was alone? He was young, wealthy, and strikingly handsome. He probably had a harem of women available at his beck and call.

All this time I'd assumed I was the only one, but perhaps that was foolish. A weight settled in the pit of my stomach.

"It's a beautiful place," I murmured absently.

Gavin continued past the den, hardly acknowledging my compliment. "I had it remodeled, gutted to the studs, before I moved in last year."

"Did you pick everything yourself?"

He nodded. "Mostly. Sonja helped too."

The woman I'd met at his office. I briefly wondered if she had a crush on him. Then again, how could she not?

"A guest room." Gavin pointed to a door on our left as he led me down a hallway. "There's a loft upstairs with a media room."

"You have a theater?"

He nodded, smiling at me. "Would you like to come over and watch a movie sometime?"

"I would love to." Somehow, I couldn't picture myself sharing a bowl of popcorn with him while a silly comedy played in the background.

Gavin pressed on, continuing the tour. "Guest bath."

"Nice."

"And the master suite." He stopped at the threshold. I guessed that this was it—the tour was over.

"Can I see?" I tried peeking around his shoulder, but the room was concealed in utter darkness.

"Where I sleep?"

I nodded.

His lips quirked up just a fraction. He was waiting for this moment. Apparently, he wanted me to be the one to ask, to give him permission for whatever was about to happen in this room.

He flipped on a small lamp on his dresser as we entered, and my eyes took a moment to adjust. It looked like a high-end hotel room.

A large iron-framed bed dressed in fluffy gray bedding was positioned between two round side tables that each held sparkling crystal lamps. A chaise lounge sat beneath the window, its velvety charcoal upholstery soft and inviting. A door led beyond to his closet and a large bathroom. It was elegant and masculine, perfectly fitting for him.

"Are you . . . seeing anyone else?" The words popped out, sounding immature and childish, even to my own ears.

His mouth tilted into a smile. "You want to know if I'm fucking someone else. Is that it, Emma?"

Biting my lower lip, I nodded.

Gavin turned to face me, taking my face in his hands. "No. I'm not. Are you?" His eyes met mine, and I could tell that my answer to this question mattered greatly to him.

"No." It was the complete truth. There was no one else but him.

"Undress," he demanded.

After a moment's hesitation, I shed my blouse and pencil skirt. With a flick of his wrist, my bra came next.

My hands moved to the hips of my panties, and I moved to pull them down until Gavin stopped me.

"Leave the panties. I want to take those off myself."

I paused, weighing his words.

"Good girl," he said, taking my breasts into his hands and sending my heart spiraling.

Letting my eyes close briefly, I steeled myself and my strength for what was to come.

Then his mouth crashed urgently against mine. Fiery sparks exploded beneath my closed eyes, and in that moment, I would have given him anything he asked for.

He kissed my lips, then trailed hot kisses down my neck while I rubbed my pelvis against his. His arousal felt so big and so hard, it could have been a baseball bat.

"Gavin . . ." The groan ripped from my throat as raw need raced through me. I clung to his powerful shoulders for support as the urgency of my need made me dizzy.

"Open my pants, Emma."

I obeyed at once, pulling down the zipper to his gray trousers and letting the weight of his belt pull them to his knees.

"Touch me," he commanded, his voice filled with more need than I'd ever heard before.

I brought my palm to his shaft and stroked the length of it, savoring the velvety feel of his hot skin.

"Use both hands."

Fisting him in both hands, I pumped up and down more firmly this time.

"There," he said, his voice controlled and measured. "Like that."

He pushed my panties down my thighs, and they fell to my ankles.

While my hands continued to work his large shaft up and down, Gavin placed his index finger in my mouth. Once I had wet it with my tongue, sucking lightly, he brought his hand between my legs, rubbing my own saliva on the sensitive bundle of nerves with feather-light touches, teasing me until I was moaning and rocking my hips toward his hand.

As we remained rooted to the center of the bedroom,

I couldn't help but wonder if we'd lie together in his bed. Surely, he didn't mean for us to have sex right here on the floor.

"On your knees, pet."

Sinking to my knees on the plush carpeting before him, I waited, my eyes watching Gavin's.

He pumped himself in long, lazy strokes, watching me with a dark, lust-filled gaze. Then he placed the broad head of his cock against my lips.

"Open for me."

I obeyed. My mouth created a warm, wet suction over his flared head, and I could feel his eyes on me, watching, surveying my work.

Licking and sucking against him, my mouth made obscene noises, and occasionally I'd let out a little moan. Gavin stayed still and quiet. Ever controlled, ever calm.

Pleasuring him felt like a gift, a privilege. He'd made me work to earn his trust, always holding a part of himself back, and now, here in his bedroom, he was more mine than he'd ever been before.

Gavin's large palms on either side of my face forced my mouth deeper onto his cock. "All of it."

"So bossy," I murmured around a mouthful of cock.

"You like it."

He was right. It was almost as if I couldn't become aroused without his barking commands. Poor Cooper never stood a chance. Dear God, why was I thinking about Cooper while Gavin's cock was halfway down my throat? I was pretty sure I needed therapy. But then Gavin surged forward, pushing past my gag reflex, and all thoughts of the younger Kingsley were forgotten.

Forcing a breath through my nose, I relaxed my throat. I was aroused, slightly alarmed. And a whole lot turned on.

Gavin was so patient, too much so, while I felt ready to combust.

"Good girl," he said. "Love the way you suck me off."

Just when I began to wonder if this was the only thing on this evening's agenda, Gavin pulled me to my feet, his hot erection pulsing between us.

"Turn around." His voice was raw, urgent.

I faced the bed and Gavin pressed his chest against my back, the wall of firm muscle guiding me to the edge of the mattress where I bent forward, resting my upper body on the bed while he loomed over me.

I heard the tear of a condom packet and imagined him wrestling a condom onto that beast of a cock. No easy feat, to be sure.

A sharp smack sliced through the silence as his palm made contact with my ass.

Rather than flinch, my instinct was to moan and push back against him. Gone was the meek little librarian. Gavin made me wanton and reckless.

"Lift your ass for me, baby," he growled.

Oh.

I arched my back, offering myself up to him, knowing his gaze caressed my private areas that were on display for him.

As demanding as he was, his cock was even more impatient, pushing forward and invading my body in a firm thrust. He continued inching forward, and I waited to feel him bottom out.

I gasped. "Jesus, Gavin. That all of it?"

"Just a little more. You'll get used to it."

I whimpered softly, my head moving from side to side as I gripped his duvet.

"It's a blessing and a curse," he said through gritted teeth, a hint of amusement in his voice.

It might have been our first time, but apparently, that didn't mean Gavin was going to take it easy on me. The sex was rough, almost brutal, like he was working out his demons on me, like he had to erase all that vulnerability he'd shown.

Pressing hot kisses between my shoulder blades, Gavin hovered over me, his hips continuing to work their magic.

Though my head was spinning, processing, my body loved his total and complete domination.

"Should have pushed you from my mind after I first saw you. Fuck. You shouldn't be here, pretty girl. Don't deserve you."

I wanted to tell him he was wrong, that he deserved love and admiration, but it was all I could do to hang on, grasping the bed as he pounded into me again and again.

My body clenched around him, and I came with a cry.

Gavin followed—gripping my ass in both palms as he let out a low grunt and emptied himself into the condom, his cock jerking inside me as my muscles continued to spasm.

When it was done, he leaned over me once more and pressed a soft kiss between my shoulder blades. "Stay put."

Moments later, he was back with a warm cloth, wiping between my legs. The moment was so unexpected and tender. Tears stung my eyes as Gavin helped me to my feet, and we each dressed in silence.

A heaviness hung in the room around us that wasn't there before, and I couldn't shake the feeling that something was wrong.

I didn't expect him to pull me into his arms for a

cuddle session, necessarily, but he hadn't even given me the privilege of laying me down on his bed, kissing or holding me while made love. He'd just bent me over the edge of it and had his way with me. But before I had time to fully process that, Gavin led me toward the hall.

"My driver will take you home now."

I paused, balling my fists at my sides. "That's it? After everything we shared today?"

"I don't know what to tell you. This is who I am, Emma."

"But you took me to see where you grew up, the restaurant ... the intimacy tonight. I thought things between us were turning into something real."

Gavin's reserved demeanor was back, his gaze icy and cold. "This isn't one of your storybooks. I never promised you a happy ending."

As we stood beside the front door, I put on my shoes and grabbed my purse. "Cooper never made me feel like this." I hurled the insult at Gavin with all the force I could muster, hoping since nothing else seemed to matter, the one thing that might would be his own sense of pride.

A flash of jealousy broke through his steely gaze before he blinked, and then it was gone in a flash. "Then maybe you should go and spend more time with him."

With tears stinging my eyes, I fled, stabbing the button for the elevator.

"Ben will meet you downstairs," Gavin said just as the elevator doors slid closed.

As if I needed one more reason to stay away from him, his cold and callous behavior tonight had sealed the deal.

Despite what he'd said, he had let me in today—however briefly. And it was magical. What else did I want? A relationship? Marriage? I almost choked on the word. Men like Gavin didn't tie themselves down to one woman for all of eternity.

He was arrogant, cold, and incredibly frustrating. The way his powerful body moved, the way my skin heated when I was near him, I craved all of it. I wished I didn't, wished desperately that I was stronger. But Gavin Kingsley had a hold over me unlike any I'd ever experienced.

Which was exactly why I needed to get out now—while I still could.

Ben opened the car door, and I slid inside just as a broken sob slipped from my throat.

Chapter Twenty-Five

Emma

I do love nothing in the world so well as you—is not that strange?

The great William Shakespeare was one of my best friends, and his *Much Ado About Nothing* was a favorite.

I was curled up on my couch under a blanket, reading, and struggling to keep my brain off the fact that I kept failing at this whole romance thing. Hard. Was it possible that I only attracted men who were all wrong for me?

Gavin had begun to let me in—only to slam the door cruelly on our relationship when it started getting a little too real for him.

Still feeling hurt after our last encounter a few days ago, I'd retreated a bit. After I talked it over with Bethany, she agreed a little space might be a good thing. Since that night, Gavin hadn't called, hadn't texted, and I had no idea where his head was at.

My mind swirled with thoughts of not only Gavin, but my last relationship before him.

When I thought back to my time with my ex, my heart hurt. Nathan had always been rough—rough kisses, rough sex—but he'd never been violent. Until he was. Shoved me down the stairs after a stupid argument, then spent the next hour working me over until he was breathless and I was a bloody mess, unable to stand on my own two feet. As soon as he left, I dialed 911, and vowed I'd never get involved with a man like him ever again.

And my greatest fear, more than falling for Gavin, was falling for Gavin and having him turn out just like Nathan.

I was in for the night, licking my wounds and trying to think about anything but the man my heart still yearned for, despite everything. Which was why the knock at my door at nine that night was unexpected.

Setting my book on the cushion beside me, I rose

from the couch. Another knock sounded on my door, louder this time.

"Emma!" a man shouted as he pounded firmly again with his fist.

For a moment, I couldn't place that voice. But when I did, icy chills snaked down my spine.

Nathan.

Frozen in place, I dared a peek through the peephole.

"I know you're in there, Emma. Let me in. We need to talk."

"There's nothing to talk about. Go away!" I called back.

"I miss you. Want you back, sweet Emma."

Not a chance in hell.

I should have never trusted him, never given him my heart in the first place, and there was no way I was ever going down that path again. The entire time we were together was a sham. I'd thought he was mine, but in reality, he was a total player, dating his way through half the city while I stayed home, missing him.

When I finally confronted him, he said a woman couldn't expect monogamy in this day and age. Yet he'd demanded it from me. Funny how that worked. And then he'd gone from dominating to controlling to downright scary in a matter of months.

The last time, he beat me so badly, I spent a week in the hospital eating my food through a tube. That had been the final straw.

Summoning my strength, I tried my most intimidating voice. "I've called the police, Nate. Get out of here and don't come back."

He grumbled something unintelligible under his breath, but moments later, I saw his form retreat away from my door and toward the street beyond.

With shaking hands, I grabbed my phone from the counter and then hesitated. My instinct had been to call Gavin, to beg him to come over and stay the night. But as my heart rate slowed, I thought it over. Based on our last interaction and the way things ended when I left his apartment, I didn't feel quite right calling him. He'd behaved like an ass, and I didn't want to call him begging him to rescue me.

Instead, I dialed Cooper, silently praying that he'd pick up.

"Princess!" his deep voice boomed, excitement radiating from it.

"Cooper," I choked out, and my voice broke.

"What is it?" His excitement was replaced by concern.

"Can you come over?" I sniffed.

"Did something happen?"

I filled him in on the unwelcome visit from my violent ex.

"I'm on my way. Keep the doors locked, and if he comes back, call the police."

"Okay."

Restless, I paced the house, still in shock that Nathan had shown up here. I hadn't heard from him in months. I probably should have called the police, but I didn't feel like waiting half the night for the city cops to show up, and then spending my evening answering questions and filling out paperwork. I knew from experience there wasn't much they could do.

A short time later, a soft knock came at my door.

"Emma? It's Cooper."

As soon as I opened the door, Cooper pulled me into his arms, hugging me tightly to his massive, muscled chest. I sagged against him, instantly relieved.

"I'm here now. You're safe," he murmured.

When he finally released me, we went to the couch and settled in side by side.

"How are you doing?" he asked.

I blew out a frustrated breath. I wanted to open up, to share all the depressing bits of my life, even though I knew he was just asking about Nathan. And his visit had rattled me, it had, but it was nothing compared to the deep ache in my soul over Gavin's rejection after the night we made love.

"You can tell me, princess. I won't judge."

I'd been sliced raw by Gavin, and I desperately needed the perspective of someone who knew him.

"What's up with your brother?"

Cooper chuckled. "Why do I know you're not talking about Quinn?"

I rolled my eyes. Of course, my mind had once again wandered to Gavin. It seemed that the more determined I was to stay away from him, the more I yearned for him. Foolish, I know.

"What are you referring to, princess?"

I leaned in closer, enjoying the body heat we shared in the chilly living room. Cooper always made me feel safe, like I could tell him anything. It was refreshing, especially after all the secrets lurking between Gavin and me that remained unspoken.

"He's just so infuriating. Has he always been like this?"

"Like what?" Cooper cocked his head, studying me as he tucked a lock of hair behind my ear.

"The man is about as in tune with his emotions as a mosquito."

Cooper chuckled again and dropped the lock of hair

he'd been toying with. "That's just the way he operates. Has been since ... fuck, I think high school, if I had to guess. Now, tell me what's going on."

"We had sex," I finally blurted.

Cooper cleared his throat. "I see." After a moment's silence, he asked, "And what? He didn't live up?"

I turned to see his mouth quirk up a fraction, and I chucked a pillow at him. "No, not that. It's just ... well, he had Ben drive me home straight after, like it was nothing more than a meaningless hookup."

"I'm sorry, Emma."

He used my name rather than the playful nickname he normally called me, and I knew it was because he truly was sorry.

"Do you think he's slept with a lot of women?" My question came out of left field, but Cooper didn't bat an eye. I loved that about him, how he never judged me. He rolled with every punch, including my insatiable hunger for his brother.

"I don't know his number, if that's what you're asking."

I shook my head. "I figured. I'm just curious . . ."

"I'm sure this isn't what you want to hear, but I told you I'd never lie to you. So, yeah, I'm fairly certain that over the years he's been with an astronomical number of women. Most of them didn't matter. Women to him were just a way to blow off steam."

My stomach sank like I'd swallowed a piece of lead. Every new thing I learned about Gavin told me to run far, far away, and yet at the same time, the pull to get closer was stronger than ever. Stupid as it was, somewhere in the back of my mind was the notion that maybe I'd be the woman to change him.

"I figured as much." The knot in my throat was impossible to disguise. Cooper knew I was upset, but he continued sitting quietly beside me, each of us studying the TV that played on mute before us.

"Maybe it doesn't have to be Gavin, princess."

I looked into his eyes, and the tenderness I saw there almost gutted me. My brain knew Cooper was the safe choice. But my heart? My heart yearned for Gavin.

"Maybe you could try . . ." His voice was

uncharacteristically soft, and my heart squeezed.

Try. I knew what he meant. Try to open my heart. Try to forget the dominating Gavin who was all wrong for me. Try to give my heart to Cooper instead.

Swallowing against my suddenly dry throat, I shook my head. "I have been trying."

That sad truth was something that neither of us wanted to face—that on paper, Cooper and I were perfect for each other. He loved literary classics and had an impressive library. He was tender, sweet, and gentle with me, all the things I knew I needed, especially after my last brutal relationship. But he was none of the things I *wanted*.

I craved Gavin's harsh brand of love. His steely persona I had to work to uncover, his presence and intensity that only intrigued me more. I was beguiled with him. It wasn't a switch I could turn off—if it were, heaven knew, I would have. I knew Gavin wasn't healthy for me, and yet, he was all I wanted.

I suddenly felt so cruel for stringing Cooper along this entire time. "I'm so sorry," I said, my eyes stinging with unshed tears.

His finger on my lips stopped me. "You have nothing to be sorry for." His tone was sweet, but his words lacked the sincerity I'd come to love from him.

I gave his hand a squeeze.

"If he hurts you, so help me God. You let me know, okay? I'll be there in a heartbeat to make it all better."

"I will." And I knew what he said was true. Cooper would be there for me if I needed him.

A little while later, Cooper left, and shortly after that, my phone rang.

It was Gavin. I couldn't help but wonder if Cooper had called him and reamed him out for the insensitive way he'd behaved, and told him about my surprise visit from Nathan. I hoped Gavin felt bad—it served him right if he did.

"Did you need something?" I asked, my tone icy.

Gavin hesitated for a long moment, and then his voice dropped low and silky. "Are you okay?"

"I am now. Cooper came over."

A slight pause. "Good. I wanted to let you know I've

made some calls, and Nathan won't be bothering you anymore."

Gavin's tone was so resolute, so final, relief instantly flooded me.

I sagged against my sofa. "Thank you. Is that all?"

"No, I'd like for you to come over tomorrow night. Are you free?"

"I'm free. What time?"

"Eight o'clock. I'll send a car."

"Okay. Good night, Gavin."

"Good night, pet."

Chapter Twenty-Six

Emma

As I dressed casually in a pair of jeans and a cable-knit sweater, I steeled my nerves, preparing myself for anything. Which man was I going to get tonight? The ultra-romantic one who whisked me off in a helicopter to a swanky winery, or the cold, calculating man who took control of my body and fucked me senseless?

Ben saw me to the elevator and then disappeared, going off to do whatever it was he did when he wasn't at Gavin's beck and call.

When the door opened, Gavin stood there, all six feet three inches of him, looking delectable in a pair of dark-washed jeans and a white tee shirt. His long feet were bare and the tops were dusted with fine hairs. I'd never seen him so casual.

"Thank you for coming," he said, ushering me inside.

But I knew one thing for sure. It didn't matter how sexy he looked, how sweetly he behaved—tonight would not end in sex.

I cleared my throat. "So . . . what's on the agenda tonight?"

"Since you seemed to appreciate the idea of using the media room . . ."

"We're watching a movie?"

He nodded. "I figured you'd enjoy some of the classics, based on your love of reading the old classics."

A *Netflix and chill* night had been the last thing I was expecting, but I was pleasantly surprised.

In the kitchen, we each grabbed a bottle of sparkling mineral water, and Gavin led the way upstairs.

His media room would have been the envy of any design magazine. The walls were painted a deep navy, and a brass chandelier hung from the ceiling, giving the room a dreamy ambience. Rich otter-colored microfiber sofas, plush tufted ottomans, and the softest cream-colored carpet I'd ever felt under my feet completed the picture.

But I couldn't allow myself to fall under his spell just yet. We had a lot of talking to do, and if I had things my way, he had some groveling to do.

As I lowered myself to the couch, I straightened my shoulders. "We need to talk."

He nodded. "I know. I owe you a massive apology."

"I'm listening."

Gavin smirked. "Sending you away after we had sex—"

"Made love," I said, correcting him.

He cleared his throat as though something was lodged there. "Made love." The words sounded foreign on his tongue, like he'd never spoken them before. "Fucked, whatever you want to call it."

I raised my eyebrows.

"It was wrong to send you away after."

"Then why did you?"

He took my hands in his, turning to fully face me on the sofa. "I've never had anything like this. Never felt this connected to anyone before. I've been trying to give you more, trying to let you in."

"Like showing me your childhood home."

"Yes. That."

I scooted closer to him on the sofa, softening already. "I appreciated that, Gavin. So much. It helps me understand you."

He nodded. "I'm trying. I promise you, I am. Just be patient with me, okay?"

"Apology accepted. But . . ."

His eyebrows drew up. "But?"

"I have a few stipulations first."

Looking amused, Gavin motioned for me to continue. "Go on."

"If we continue this—seeing each other—I need to know what we are."

"Like a label?" he asked, looking even more amused.

My cheeks heated. "Yes, I'd like to know what this is."

"The word boyfriend is too juvenile, Emma. I'm a thirty-four-year-old man. I'm yours, and you're mine. That good enough for you?"

I nodded. "So, you're my person?"

"Your person?"

"My person. My plus-one, the person I can count on."

"Yes, I'm your person," he confirmed

"And we're monogamous?"

"Of course. I'm very much a one-woman kind of man. Always have been."

That soothed my ragged nerves somewhat.

"What else?" he asked. "Any more rules?"

"Yes. Just one more. I'm not asking to stay the night—not yet, anyway—but after sex, I'd like to cuddle. Lie in bed together. Talk. Kiss. That kind of thing," I added, suddenly feeling shy.

"Okay. But I have one rule of my own."

"What is it?"

"I don't want you riding the bus to work anymore. You'll either allow me to buy you a car or hire a driver for you."

"Gavin, absolutely not. I can't allow you to buy me a car, or have someone cart me around."

He raised his palm to silence me. "I agreed to every one of your stipulations without argument. Give this to me, Emma."

"We'll revisit it next month."

"Next week."

"Fine," I conceded.

His mouth crashed against mine, urgent and demanding.

"God, I missed you," he murmured, peppering my mouth with kisses.

Sweet relief flooded through me. Gavin's mood changes were giving me whiplash. But despite all that, I was happy. Truly happy.

"Movie time?" he asked, straightening the erection in his jeans.

I could have choked on my laugh if I weren't so aroused. "Yes. Movie time."

He read me the choices and we settled on *Casablanca*. I'd never seen it before, and he said it was one of his favorites. We shared sugary candy and cuddled on the couch while the movie played.

And for the next two hours, it was utter perfection. Everything a date with your *person* was supposed to be.

• • •

"Give me that mouth." Gavin groaned, his voice tense, and I closed the distance, sealing my lips over his.

He had carried me to his bedroom when the movie ended. I'd been sleepy at first, but now I was anything but.

Shedding his clothes quickly, Gavin joined me on the bed. Pushing my jeans and panties down my legs, he lowered his mouth to my belly, my thighs, and kissed each inch of skin he exposed.

Moments later, he was pushing inside me, making me cry out.

This was what I'd imagined our first time would be—face-to-face, heartbeat to heartbeat, his kisses at my throat, my hands gripping his powerful shoulders.

It was heaven. Way too soon, I exploded around him in a breath-stealing orgasm.

"That's it, baby. Love it when you come for me."

Gavin brought his mouth to mine, treating me to soft kisses while I rode out the aftershocks of my release. Gripping my hip, he lifted my leg around his ribs, angling himself even deeper.

"Fuck. You're perfect," he murmured.

He continued pumping in and out in measured strokes, and though I'd already come once, I still wanted more.

I reached between my legs, desperate for more contact, my fingers moments away from finding the spot that so desperately needed attention.

"What do you think you're doing?" Gavin's voice was a harsh pant.

I paused, frowning up at him. "I want to come again."

"Too bad. This isn't for you. It's for me." Pinning my wrists above my head, he slammed home, taking me in one powerful thrust.

I gasped, my lungs heaving for oxygen.

"Just lay there like a good little girl while I take what's mine."

Mine.

And I was.

I was totally and completely his.

Chapter Twenty-Seven

Gavin

"That's it, pet. Take what I give you." I rocked my hips into Emma's, setting a steady pace.

I loved pushing her boundaries, watching her give in and give up control.

She let out a sharp gasp, but brought her legs around my waist.

The night I sent her away, I'd woken up in soaking-wet sheets, drenched in a cold sweat and fearful that I'd just sent away the one good thing in my life. My chest felt like it had been split in two.

It was sheer luck that she'd agreed to come back to me. And with some rules of her own too. Her backbone was inspiring. She wasn't some pushover submissive ... my girl had spirit.

And she accepted me, flaws and all.

I drew up on my knees, appreciating the view of Emma spread out before me, and continued pumping in long, measured strokes.

Her chest heaving, her lips slightly parted, her tits bouncing with each thrust, she was beautiful. Her eyes sparkled on mine.

"You okay?" I asked.

She gave me a tight nod.

"Good. Because I could do this all night."

My lust rising, I drove harder, gripping her luscious ass in both hands. The position forced me deeper, and I felt Emma's body clench tightly around me.

"Coming again?" I whispered against her neck.

A small whimper and the nod of her head against my throat were the only answers I got before her tight opening clenched wildly, milking my cock.

A deep groan of satisfaction rose in my throat. I buried myself to the hilt one last time, my release ripping through me with ferocity.

After I ditched the condom and cleaned us up, I returned to the bed where Emma had made herself comfortable beneath the sheets.

As we lay together, skin to skin, hard muscle against

soft curves, I enjoyed the heat of her body against mine. I'd denied myself this simple pleasure for so long, somewhere deep down afraid of getting too attached. But, fuck it, I was already in too far. Now, I might as well see this thing through until the end.

My head was spinning with unanswered questions about where all this would lead. I didn't have the best track record, and knew I'd inevitably find a way to fuck this up.

As Emma lay curled in my arms, so soft and trusting, I couldn't help my mind from wandering to more sinister things, like what happened to Ashley might happen to Emma if I wasn't careful.

I clutched her tighter, not wanting to face reality just yet.

Chapter Twenty-Eight

Gavin

I didn't like this. Not one fucking bit. In fact, under normal circumstances, I might have stopped the car and demanded to get out.

But considering I had no idea where we were or where we were going, and Emma was looking at me so intently ... her cheeks pink, her eyes glowing with excitement? Well, it seemed like a dick move to try to back out now. And besides, the more time I spent with her, the harder it was to say no. To all her little rules.

That fact alone should have made me bolt in the opposite direction, but for some reason, my ass was glued to the seat.

"Why won't you tell me where we're going?" I asked.

"Ben knows. Isn't that enough?" she teased.

"No. Ben won't tell me anything either."

"That's because Ben and I have an understanding." She grinned. "Besides, since when were you the only one who got to plan special surprise dates? Can't I do something nice for you in return?"

I considered that. It was a sensible question, but that didn't make the answer easy to swallow. I wasn't good at accepting gestures of affection. Never had been. So, while I understood on an intellectual level the need to do it, I felt twitchy about the whole thing in a way I couldn't shake. Especially now. Especially with Emma. After our past few dates, each as sexy as hell but also intimate in ways I had been trying not to think about, I knew I was in too deep. But, damn if I could bring myself to pull away.

"Can't you at least give me a clue?"

"I swear, you're like a little kid. Just relax." She chuckled. "You don't have to shake the box to figure out what's inside."

"I know what's inside." I moved closer and ran my palm along her smooth, exposed inner thigh, but she slapped my hand away.

"It's not that kind of surprise," she said. I was slightly mollified that her voice was just a little breathless.

"And what if I want it to be? Do we have time?" I nipped her earlobe and she began to laugh, but just as she writhed under my touch, the car jolted to a halt.

"We're here?" I asked, craning to see out the window, but Emma grabbed me by the lapel and forced me back.

"I get out first," she said.

"You will not—"

"When I get out, you might get a peek up my dress," she purred.

Beaten by that logic, I leaned back on the plush cushions and waited as she bent over me, flashing the frill of her lavender panties as she climbed from the car. Then, when the space was clear, I followed her into a parking lot that was filled with gravel rather than pavement.

The building in front of us was so big, it might have been a warehouse in another life. Huge, glowing letters read FAMILY FUN PALACE in colorful bright neon.

Son of a bitch. What had I gotten myself into?

"You brought me to . . . what? Babysit?"

"Nope." Grinning, she shook her head. "This whole place is ours for the day."

I frowned. "What?"

"You were being so thoughtful with your classic-movie night and your wine tasting, and I figured . . . well, this is probably something you never got the chance to do when you were little. When I was seven, I went to a place like this and broke my tooth riding bumper cars with my cousin Miranda. It's an important experience in a kid's life, this kind of stuff," she said, her expression grave. "This is the type of place you make memories."

I raised my eyebrows, trying not to grin at the thought of a young, freckle-nosed Emma with a chipped tooth, and failing. "Is that so?"

"It is. Dingy rides, squeaky bolts that may or may not have been checked this decade, one-eyed carnies leering at you. It's a rite of passage. And today, at this arcade, you are going to have it," she said, her eyes blazing with determination.

"I'm not going to ride bumper cars with a bunch of ten-year-olds and—"

"We won't have to. This place is ours. Totally. I bought it out for the day. Bethany's uncle owns it, and he gave me a good deal. So, come on. No more excuses. What are you waiting for?"

She held her hand out to me just as the gray sky above us started spitting rain, and I didn't have time to think of a way out. I closed my hand over hers, and we rushed inside the huge metal doors as quickly as we could manage before the downpour began.

It was only once we were inside that I realized exactly how much work she must have put in. At every stall, men and women were waiting for us, smiling while we decided where to walk, and a massive speaker played old nineties hits, songs that I knew from my childhood.

Standing back, I shook my head. "This must have cost you a fortune." As I automatically tallied up the cost of this many people's time, it hit me that she'd probably dropped a whole night's pay on this date. Money she could have used fixing up her beloved brownstone.

Instead, she'd spent it on me. The man who had everything, and nothing, all at the same time.

My throat tightened, and I cleared it with a grumble. "Look, Emma . . . you didn't have to—"

"Nobody has to do anything. I did this because I wanted to." She squeezed my hand. "Now, let's talk tickets."

Not bothering to look at me, she dragged me toward a little kiosk filled with rubber balls, plush bananas, fashion dolls, and water pistols. Each had a little tag in front of it with a price.

"We have to know what we're aiming for. You can't just go earning tickets willy-nilly."

"What do you mean?"

"I mean, pick a prize so we can get our minds right and set our goal for the day," she said. "When I was ten, my dad and I worked all day and night at a place like this to get me the knock-off Barbie doll."

"Was she your favorite toy from there on out?" I asked, genuinely curious.

She shook her head and let out a snort. "Nope. It broke the next day. Her head came clean off . . . it was a grisly scene. But it was the experience that mattered." She shrugged one slim shoulder. "Come on, pick a prize."

I glanced around. There wasn't much for adults, just

a few T-shirts with things like I'M WITH STUPID written on them. Then my gaze fell on the one thing I'd always wanted as a kid.

"They have foam-pellet guns?" I nodded toward a rack of toys complete with plastic scopes, and Emma beamed.

"Looks like we've got a winner. All we need to get is, um, three thousand tickets. Shouldn't be a problem."

I raised my eyebrows. Sounded like a problem to me. They might as well have made it a million.

"It's going to happen. All you have to do is believe and pick a game so we can get this going."

For a while, we wandered around, looking at carts of food and side attractions before I found the pit of games. There was a huge wall of Connect Four and an animatronic dinosaur game, but my eye caught on a classic and I couldn't resist.

"Skee-Ball," I said, taking her hand as we stuffed tokens into the game and balls dropped into the slot.

To my surprise, Emma had a pretty good arm on her, and for a moment I stood back and watched as she sank one ball after another.

"Well, are you going to win those tickets or not?" she teased, shooting me a challenging glance.

"Not if you're going to embarrass me with your skills. I can't compete with that."

"If you're waiting to find something here you can beat me at, it's going to be a very long day," she said with a sassy wink. "I'm what you call an arcade master. A pinball wizard. A—"

"Dork," I finished, and she stuck her tongue out at me. "Fine. I'll give it a go."

I threw my balls while I watched her from the corner of my eye, studying her form as she bent and released. Part of me was imagining what it might be like to lean over her and feel her body move with every throw, but the other part was studying her form so I could replicate it and get some fucking tickets.

I would deny it with my dying breath, but how badly I wanted that pellet gun? It was unconscionable.

Maybe because she was right. It was a symbol of everything this day was about. Never in my life had I gotten to have an afternoon like this, the chance to be a kid without worries or responsibilities. Except, of course, now it was better. Because if I'd gotten to do this all those years ago, Emma wouldn't have been beside me right now.

I managed to get the hang of Skee-Ball. Once we were done, she held up a fistful of tickets that shot out of the slot.

"Awesome," she said, eyeing the little red stubs with narrowed eyes. "That has to be at least fifty. We're on our way."

After Skee-Ball, we played a few rounds of Connect Four and a few more games that sucked away my tokens until I had to ask Emma for more with a laugh.

"How many tickets do we have now?" I asked.

She glanced in her bucket. "I'd say about five hundred."

"And what would that get us?" I asked.

"A consolation prize," she said with a decisive shake of her head. "We didn't come for that. We came for victory."

I grinned, rolling my eyes at her. "Fine, what do we do next?" I'd never been so fucking out of my element, and if Emma weren't so damn cute, I'd have called this entire thing off.

"I say we take a break and get our strength up with some good old-fashioned bumper cars." She nodded toward a little rink in the corner of the room next to a massive Ferris wheel whose lights had only just come on.

"I'm game," I said.

"When was the last time you even drove?"

"My car or my helicopter?" I countered.

She narrowed her eyes at me. "Touché."

The ride operator let us into the rink, and together we picked out our cars. For me, I picked a bright white car that reminded me of the *Speed Racer* cartoons I'd loved growing up. For Emma, a glittery pink car that would be fit for a princess . . . or a knock-off Barbie doll.

The timer ticked down and then, with a blare of music overhead, we began to move. I careened toward her, sure I was about to cause a head-on collision, just as she turned and narrowly missed my attack. I spun my wheel, ready to regroup, but not fast enough. She was backing up into me, hitting me with all the force of her back bumper and grinning like a maniac.

"I'll get you for that," I yelled.

"I'd like to see you try!"

I steered toward her again, following her around the course until my heart dropped into my stomach and the music slowed. The ride was over.

I'd never felt so much adrenaline, so much *fun* in my life. I wanted to ask her to go again, to maybe go for best two out of three, but she was climbing from her car, fixing her mussed hair and laughing.

"Okay, now that you got your butt handed to you, you ready to get some more tickets? That gun's not gonna win itself."

"Yup. Let's go." I nodded, then followed her back into the arcade toward a game where I had to throw baseballs to knock down the most haunting clowns I'd ever seen.

I couldn't say how many games we played or for how long we were there, running from one booth to the next like our asses were on fire. Every moment felt limitless, and as we raced to see who could get more layups or throw more basketballs, I again caught myself looking at her from the corner of my eye, wondering about the sort of person, the sort of woman, who would do this for another person.

Especially for a bastard like me.

"Are you hungry?" she asked when she caught me staring.

My stomach growled, though I hadn't realized I was hungry until she'd mentioned it. "Yeah, sure, let's grab something."

"The pizza here is amazing, according to Bethany."

"Pizza it is," I agreed, and we each got a slice before making our way to the Ferris wheel.

"Think they'll let us take it on?" she asked, nodding toward the ride operator.

"Only one way to find out." I hopped the gate, walked up the stairs, and called for the man's attention.

With bleary eyes, he gazed back at me. "What?"

"I was just wondering if we might be able to eat our pizza on the ride?"

He shrugged. "All the same to me. Come on up."

The carriages rolled to a stop and I spied one, bright pink and sparkly. "This one." I ushered her inside.

"Never thought you were much for pink." She grinned, then took a bite of her pizza.

"I can't believe you like olives," I said, grimacing at her slice.

"I can't believe your palate isn't refined enough to appreciate them," she shot back, grinning. "Pepperoni is so common."

"Don't knock my pepperoni."

"Then don't knock my olives."

I smiled at her. "Fine. I'll try it. Here."

We swapped slices and, holding my breath, I took a bite. Salty, oily brine filled my mouth, and it was all I could do to swallow.

Choking, I said, "Take it back. Christ, that's foul."

"See? What did I say. No appreciation." She laughed.

That was where she was dead wrong. I'd been gifted Cartier watches from girlfriends in the past. A motorcycle one Christmas from my brothers. I'd even gotten a trip to Belize from a grateful client who wound up marrying one of the escorts.

But this?

This was the best gift anyone had ever given me, hands down, and there was nothing I wanted more than to stay in this moment, on top of this Ferris wheel with Emma, overlooking the one and only day I'd ever gotten to be a kid.

My heart squeezed inside my chest. As much as I wanted to force the feelings away, I couldn't do it. This moment . . . this woman?

It was everything.

Chapter Twenty-Nine

Emma

This was the way dates should be.

A guy and a girl, eating pizza on a Ferris wheel, just enjoying the night and not worrying about what the next day would bring.

I wished there were more times like these. Times when I could forget Gavin was some multi-millionaire CEO of an escort agency. This was when I liked him best.

I didn't need the helicopters or the fancy wine tastings, as nice as they were. That was fantasy fun. More important to me were the nights with Netflix, watching *Casablanca* and enjoying the sweetness of each other's company. The total and complete contentment I had when I was with Gavin.

I wasn't sure how I was going to get him that dart gun, but as we exited the Ferris wheel and made our way back into the main arcade, I glanced at him from the corner of my eye, wondering if he'd notice if I tried to pay the guy off for the toy.

He would. Nothing around Gavin went unnoticed, so I suggested he head to the animatronic dinosaur game without me.

"You don't want to shoot rabid dinosaurs?" he challenged.

I shook my head. "That game blows steam in your face, and it's just a little too real for me."

He laughed. "Chicken."

"I'm not denying that. I have to use the bathroom, anyway. I'll meet up with you."

He hesitated for a moment, but then walked off. I studied his back for a long moment before heading in the opposite direction.

Tonight, I felt something I'd never felt before with Gavin. It wasn't just an easy comfort that was usually so lacking around him. That was nice, of course, but it was something else . . . something that, if I was honest, shook me to my core.

When I looked at him, I knew that I didn't want to be with anyone else in the world.

The feeling, *the need* was so all consuming that it scared me, but I knew what it was. I'd felt the strong grip before, and that time it had taken me down a path that almost undid me.

This was love. The strong, obsessive adoration of finding someone in the world I wanted to make happy. I would move heaven and earth to do it, and I practically had by renting out this arcade, but at the end of the day? As good as it felt?

It was dangerous. Like code-red dangerous.

I was in over my head, but more than that, like so much of my relationship with Gavin—I was completely beyond my control.

There was no way of knowing what might happen next, who he might be tomorrow, though I would love him just the same. The scariest part was not knowing how Gavin felt about me. Or if he was capable of giving in to the feeling of love at all.

There were times I would catch him looking at me, his eyes soft with something that made my heart warm and my knees weak. But it wasn't enough.

I wanted more. The big, splashy, over-the-top love. The happy ending. Even more than he wanted this damned pellet gun.

My mind reeling, I tried to get my head on straight as I made it to the prize booth and grinned at the bored-looking man behind the counter.

"Look," I said. "I know the foam dart gun costs—"

"Forty bucks."

"What?" I asked, blinking.

"My boss isn't here," he said, scratching at his stubbled chin. "I'll give it to you for forty dollars."

I pursed my lips and gave him the side-eye, sizing him up. "Sixty for two of them. Final offer."

He nodded, then pulled the guns from the case and set them on the counter beside my money. "Anything else?"

I glanced at the wad of tickets still in my hand. "What will five hundred tickets get me?"

"Temporary tattoos," he said. "They're of Care Bears."

"Perfect."

I handed over my tickets and accepted the packet of tattoos before rushing to the bathroom to grab a paper towel with cold water. Laughing at myself, I adhered the tattoo, then removed each of the guns from their packaging and loaded their ammo holsters.

Finally, I was ready. Armed with a blue Care Bear on my cheek, I rushed into battle with one gun on my hip and the other in my hand.

Luckily, Gavin wasn't hard to find. He was walking casually toward the bathrooms, looking for me, no doubt.

"What happened? You were gone for—"

I lifted my hand and fired, hitting him dead center in the chest with a foam pellet.

He laughed. "How did you—"

I shot him again, this time in the forehead.

"Do that again and I'm going to have to put you over my knee and punish you."

His dark voice sent a sweet shiver down my spine, and I was half tempted to do it again, just to see if he'd make good on his promise. Before I got the chance, though, he lunged for me and grabbed the spare gun.

I lifted my weapon to fire when he shot me in the boob.

"Constant vigilance," he warned, looking smug.

"Where was your constant vigilance when I was owning you a minute ago?"

"Everyone knows it's not honorable to shoot an unarmed man. I thought you had more class than that. I guess I was wrong." He shot me again, this time in the shoulder. "Nice bear, by the way."

"Thanks. Now, prepare to die."

I took off at a sprint in the other direction, running in a serpentine pattern, careful to duck for shelter as a foam dart whizzed past my ear.

For what felt like hours, we rushed around the arcade, shooting at each other until we were both breathless, out of ammo, and too exhausted to look for any more.

It was dark outside, and the staff had started cleaning

up. I knew what that meant and I think Gavin did too, but I wanted to stop it. To go back in time and relive this day over and over, watching the joy on his face as he played each game for the very first time.

I wasn't ready to say good-bye to today. Not yet. But then Ben texted me, letting me know he was back for our scheduled pickup, and our time was up.

Gavin found me crouched outside a photo booth and held his hand out for me. "Time to go," he said simply, and though his face was impassive, I knew he was just as affected as I was.

I nodded. "Okay."

Together, we made our way to the limo and buckled in, each grabbing a water from the mini-fridge inside. For a while, we sat in silence, staring out the window and wondering what came next, but then Gavin surprised me.

"You were right," he said. "I've never had a day like today in all my life, Emma. Thank you for that. I can't tell you what it means to me."

I offered him a soft smile. "It was my pleasure. Really."

He studied me for a long moment. "I . . . I never got the chance to do those things, you know, because my childhood wasn't normal. Not just in the way that we were too poor for vacations and arcades."

I stayed silent, knowing this was my time to listen, not to speak.

"It's difficult for me to talk about." He spread his hands wide. "But I feel like . . . Well, I want you to know. Everything."

I nodded, encouraging him to continue.

"My mother was a good woman. She did her best." He took a sip of his water, his strong throat working as he looked out the window into the night. "But she had no real skills, and three children to feed and care for."

"What about your father?"

Gavin shook his head, his gaze returning to mine. "I hardly remember him. He took off right after Cooper was born. I think I was maybe six? My mother did what she had to do to put food on the table and keep a roof over our heads."

I swallowed, nodding again. "I understand."

"You saw where we grew up—it wasn't exactly bustling with opportunity. It was all low-paying jobs and no room for advancement. But still, it took me a long time to accept that my mother worked as a prostitute."

I reached over and took Gavin's hand, the words hanging in the air between us. I couldn't even imagine the things he must have seen.

"When we were older, we'd help her where we could. We got odd jobs and would protect her from the johns when she needed it. Quinn did most of the heavy lifting, and we both did a lot to shield Cooper from whatever we could. But we were still kids, and that was all we could do. When she died . . . it was a tragedy and a relief."

I remained silent, hoping to show him with my expression how much I cared. How heartsick I was for his pain. And, most of all, how honored I was that he'd finally told me this.

"Then it was just the three of us and we only knew how to do one thing—protect women. We weren't in the market to be pimps and we didn't want to exploit anyone, but we'd been around enough casinos and nightclubs with our mother to know there was a lot of money available for a woman who was willing to look good on someone's arm." He shrugged. "So, we started Forbidden Desires. Now, of course, we make a better living than we ever dreamed of, and we don't have to worry about where our next meal is coming from. But sometimes it still feels strange to realize how far I've come, and how much all three of us and my poor mother had sacrificed to get here."

I had no words. The shock, the sadness, it was all overwhelming, threatening to consume me. I'd had guesses about what their life might have been like, but nothing came close to this. Nothing came close to the true horror of their childhood.

"I'm so sorry, Gavin."

He shook his head. "There's nothing to be sorry about. The past is in the past. But I just . . . I just wanted you to know."

"Thank you," I said softly. With a jolt, I realized we were sitting outside my brownstone, the car idling as we spoke.

I nodded toward the door. "Do you want to come

inside?"

He shook his head. "Not tonight."

Moving toward me, he cupped my cheek in his hand and pulled my lips to his, sweeping me up in the most heart-aching kiss of my life. It was soft and tender and everything Gavin wasn't. Or, at least, everything I'd thought he wasn't until now.

When we broke apart, my heart sank as I climbed from the car and made my way up the steps to my house. Rain drizzled on the cold city streets, and I watched the limo pull back onto the asphalt, zooming into the night.

Even though it was raining, I couldn't bring myself to go inside until I couldn't see the limo anymore. Like, if I just waited here on this step for a few more minutes, Gavin might come back and tell me all the other things I wanted to know.

Like whether he loved me the way that I loved him. Or whether he was capable of love at all.

It was that last part that made my chest ache with uncertainty.

Chapter Thirty

Gavin

Goddamn it.

I'd said too much.

I'd known it from the second the words left my lips, but I couldn't bring myself to regret my decision. Not even when I saw the dawning horror of realization on her delicate features. Not even now, the next morning, as I sat up in my bed and thought about the night before.

I didn't know why I hadn't gone into the house with her. After a date like that, she deserved to be taken to bed and shown just how thoroughly I appreciated her efforts. Still, I needed time to think, time to work out my feelings, and the coiled knot in my stomach that seemed to tighten that much more every time I thought of Emma needed to fucking uncoil.

These emotions were unlike the ones I'd ever had before, that much I knew. What I'd thought was love years ago paled in comparison to what I felt now. I didn't worry about Emma—I knew she could care for and protect herself. She wasn't fragile or delicate like Ashley had been.

But the rest of it? The need to know where she was and what she was doing? The need to possess her completely? That was there, rearing its ugly head and roaring like a lion for me to fulfill my aching need to be with her.

It was already nine in the morning and a Saturday, which meant I should have been in the office. Not because I had to be but because I was a creature of habit. For Emma, I knew this usually meant a day of wrangling workers at the library, psyching everyone up for their busy day while people picked out the books and videos they'd be checking out for the week.

I knew where she was and what she was doing, and that I'd likely see her later.

So, why didn't that feel like it was enough anymore?

With a groan, I moved from my bed and slipped on a button-down shirt and my favorite jeans before heading into my kitchen and grabbing a cup of coffee.

Maybe I ought to go to the library and apologize for being so frank with her, for bringing down the mood of what had otherwise been the most perfect day of my life. But then ... I didn't feel that way. I regretted the vulnerability, but not the words themselves. There had to be a way to wash that vulnerability from her mind without mentioning what I'd said last night. To bring things back into focus where I felt in control again, because right now? I was spinning out.

That was what I needed to make this ache in my gut fade, I realized with a start.

Control.

Finishing my coffee in one gulp, I texted Ben and slipped on my shoes, ready for the long ride to the library on the outskirts of town, and the woman I knew would be there when I stepped inside.

Opting for surprise, I decided not to let her know I was coming, planning instead exactly how I would execute my plan when I arrived. It would be difficult—the library would be filled with people today.

But then, that's what made it all the more exciting.

Ben pulled up and I stepped from the car, letting him know he could take his coffee break if he needed to while

I was gone. Then, with a determined smile on my face, I made my way for the wide oak doors of the library and pushed through to find a pristine hall of books, hallowed in silence, and a pretty young woman standing behind the checkout counter.

Walking toward her, I noted the color of her hair and eyes and figured this must have been Emma's friend Bethany.

"Excuse me." I cleared my throat but was careful to keep my tone hushed. "Could you tell me where I could find Emma Bell?"

Bethany blinked. "Emma? The head librarian? She's in her office. Is there something I can help you with?"

I extended my hand. "My name is Gavin Kingsley. I'm a friend of Emma's, and I was hoping to see her."

Bethany tilted her head to the side, her eyes brightening as she took my hand in hers. "So nice to meet you, Gavin. I'll get her right away."

Picking up the black phone beside her computer, she dialed a number and then said, "Emma, someone is here to see you." Then, after a pause, "You'll just have to come and find out."

Not waiting for a response, Bethany put down the phone and turned her grin on me. "Emma will be out in a few seconds. Her office is right down the hall."

And there Emma was, striding down an aisle of books and looking a little put out. That was, until she saw my face.

Then, almost like magic, she relaxed and turned a smile on both me and her friend. "What a great surprise. Gavin, come in. Well, you're already in. But I mean . . . wow. You're here. At my work."

From the corner of my eye, I saw Bethany waggle her eyebrows, and I swallowed a laugh. "I hope that's not a problem."

"Of course not. I just have a few things to finish up in my office, and then we can, um, go to lunch if you want. Come this way."

She shot her friend a wide-eyed look that I didn't miss, and then I followed her back down the row of reference books until we reached an ornate old alcove with a frosted-glass door stenciled with her name and title in gold and black letters.

"Swanky digs," I said, and she rolled her eyes.

"It's okay."

"Nonsense. You're very important around here." I stepped past her into the office, rounding her huge wood desk and taking a seat in her rolling leather chair. "Shut the door."

She raised her eyebrows, her cheeks flushing a pretty pink. "You know, I happen to be the boss around here."

"You stopped being the boss the moment I walked into this building, and you and I both know it," I replied coolly.

She snapped the door closed and pulled the blinds, then, with the click of a latch, she locked the door behind her.

"Good girl," I said. "I wanted to thank you for a job well done yesterday."

She wet her lips as she surveyed me. "Is that so?"

I nodded. "It is. And since you were such a good little date planner, I'm going to let you ride my cock.

Would you like that?"

Her breath caught as she blinked at me. "H-here? In the library?"

"No place better." I grinned as my shaft swelled at the thought. "Now, undress for me."

She glanced over her shoulder at the door and then straightened. "You first," she shot back.

"Talk back to me like that again and I'll take away your privileges," I muttered.

Without another word, she set to work unbuttoning her blouse. Slowly, button by button, she showed me more of her supple, creamy skin, the lace of her white bra, until finally her shirt dropped to the floor and she reached behind her to unfasten her skirt and let it fall into a pool at her feet.

With a rush of satisfaction, I realized she wore the sort of stockings that needed a garter belt, and when she reached to unfasten its clips, I held up a hand to stop her.

"Leave those on," I demanded, my chest going tight with desire. "And be very careful not to get a run in those black stockings. I think you'll need them again in the very near future."

She grinned. "But what about my panties?"

"I'll push those aside. Take off your bra and let me see those gorgeous tits."

She didn't need to be told twice. With a twist of the wrist, her bra fell to the floor and she stepped toward me, still in her shiny leather pumps. "Do you want me to take off my shoes?"

I shook my head, then pulled down my jeans and boxers in one tug, settling myself back in the chair as my cock sprang free.

Then, just as she had done, I pulled off my shirt slowly, showing her my chest muscle by muscle, inch by inch. As I did, her pink little tongue darted out to wet her lips again before she finally bit down on her bottom lip and sank to her knees in front of me.

"No, I said you're going to ride my cock, not taste it," I said, though I'd be lying if I said the needy look in her eyes didn't make me harder than a fucking baseball bat.

Nodding, she stood again and then straddled me. I

shoved her panties aside, showing me her pretty pink pussy as her thighs opened for me.

Her skin against mine sent a thrill of need through me and I gripped my shaft, working it up and down as I stared at her slick pink center.

"Touch yourself for me. Then, when you're ready to come, I want you to come around my cock. Understand?" I managed to murmur through gritted teeth.

She nodded, then allowed her hand to drift between her thighs, massaging gently for me as her fingers slid lower. With slow, steady circles, she worked her sensitive bud until her nipples drew tight into straining peaks.

Careful not to interrupt her, I took one of those pink nipples into my mouth, rolling my tongue around the tip between sucking deep and releasing her with a groan.

"You're going to make me scream in the library," she whispered.

"Every time you want to scream, bite your lip for me. Or whisper my name."

Her eyes darkened, and the slow, steady circles around her clit quickened to forceful, demanding strokes.

Likewise, I gripped myself tighter, pumping myself in lazy strokes, pausing only to grab a condom from my jeans.

"Will you put that on for me?" she whispered.

"Are you getting close, baby?"

She nodded, her breaths coming in pants. "I feel like I'm going to . . ."

She bit hard on her lip, and I tore open the foil packet before quickly rolling the rubber over my aching shaft. Gripping her hips in my hand, I forced her down on top of me and she gasped, her eyes practically crossing as she threw her head back.

"Gavin." Her whisper may as well have been a scream for all the need it conveyed.

Her pussy was quaking, begging for release, and I gripped her hips harder as I moved her up and down on top of me.

"Play with your nipples for me, baby," I said, and she did.

Taking each of her breasts in hand, she rolled her thumbs over her straining peaks, giving me the perfect view of her bouncing chest as I worked her toward climax. Every muscle in my body was tensing, begging for release, but I held back, watching her bite her lip so hard, I was sure she might draw blood while her pussy quaked and twitched around me.

This was it. In this moment, she was completely and totally mine. As I continued to work her body up and down over mine, my biceps strained and my heart beat hard and fast. When I brought my mouth to hers, our tongues collided, and the intensity of the moment finally caught up with us.

Her body clenched around me, squeezing me to the point of pain before she collapsed onto my chest. I felt wave after wave of her searing ecstasy as she rode me.

She took everything I had to give and more, and when I knew she was in the final moment of her release, I joined her, holding my breath and loving every second of the sweet relief that flooded my body. My cock jerked and bucked, hot liquid spurting in jets as I quaked beneath her.

It was over in a matter of minutes, and me?

All I could think of was when we could do it again.

Because I was crazy in love with Emma Bell.

Chapter Thirty-One

Emma

"Thanks for doing this," Cooper said, pulling open the door for me to enter ahead of him.

The furniture store was a thirty-minute drive from the city, and during it, Cooper and I managed to talk about anything but Gavin. I was immensely proud of myself because if I allowed my brain to go there, all I'd be able to think about was the incredibly hot way he took me in the library the other day.

"Of course," I said, taking in the beautiful surroundings. The store specialized in outdoor furniture, and Cooper had pleaded with me, saying he wanted to redecorate his balcony and needed a woman's touch. Naturally, I'd been game to come along.

We wandered through the store for a moment, getting our bearings.

"This is nice," Cooper said, leaning over a sleek concrete bar top with built-in stools. It was so masculine and oversized. Honestly, the thing was hideous.

Taking his arm, I steered him away from it. "First, we need to determine what your goals are for the space."

His eyebrows jerked up. "My goals?"

"Yes." I wandered toward a cluster of outdoor sofas. "Like how you envision using your balcony."

Cooper's gaze turned thoughtful. He sank onto one of the plush conversation sets, and I sat next to him. "Honestly, someplace to just chill. Something comfortable where I can unwind."

"Maybe somewhere to entertain a special lady friend?" I winked at him.

"Sure. A cool date spot. That's a good idea. And someplace I can hang out with my brothers on the weekend with some cocktails."

I nodded. "How about this?" I pointed to a sectional sofa in slate gray.

He considered it, wandering over and sinking down onto the cushions. "This is perfect."

And it was. It was large enough to accommodate him

and his brothers, and sleek and modern enough to look handsome on his balcony.

Next, we selected a coffee table, a steel drum that could be used as an end table, and an iron-and-glass bar cart.

"How about a rug?" I asked, stopping in front of a selection of outdoor rugs.

"Whatever you think."

"Something soft underfoot would be nice. It would define the space under the sectional." After looking through the choices, I selected a cream-colored chunky knit rug that looked sturdy but still felt cozy.

"Perfect. Thanks for doing this, Emma." Cooper's gaze met mine, and I could tell he was genuinely grateful.

"Now comes the fun part. We get to accessorize."

Cooper chuckled at me. "I didn't know my balcony needed accessories."

"Of course it does. Good thing you have me." As I said it, I instantly felt bad. The truth was, Cooper didn't have me. He didn't have anyone. He was a sweet guy and deserved someone special, and I couldn't help but wonder if at one time, he'd thought that person might be me.

Pushing those thoughts from my brain, I helped him select a few things that would make the space feel cozy—a potted plant, a couple of large lanterns and candles, and several accent pillows in a soft pattern of cream, mustard yellow, and slate gray to tie the space together.

We hauled everything to the front of the store where Cooper handed over his credit card without even bothering to look at any of the price tags. *Must be nice.*

After our shopping spree, Cooper loaded up his SUV, and we set off back toward the city.

"You want to grab something to eat before I drop you off?" he asked.

"I'm sorry, I can't. I have plans after this."

"With Gavin?"

We'd successfully avoided mentioning his name all day, but now that we had, it was as if a floodgate of emotion had been unleashed inside me. Butterflies danced inside my belly, and nervous anticipation about seeing Gavin again washed over me. We were growing closer than ever, and though I didn't know what our future held, I was holding out hope that he could finally commit to a real relationship.

"No, actually. My friend Bethany is coming over later." I grabbed my phone from my purse to see if she'd texted me yet. Nothing.

"How are things, um, going?" Cooper cleared his throat and gripped the steering wheel tighter. "With Gavin, I mean," he forced out.

Peering straight ahead, I clasped my hands in my lap. "Things have been . . . progressing."

Cooper's hands tightened further still. "That's good, right?"

I let out a sharp breath. "Yes, but sometimes I still feel so unsure about us. Sometimes knowing how he truly feels is still a mystery to me."

Cooper nodded. "Totally get that. Gavin's guarded with his emotions. He always has been. Shit, I think I remember having this same conversation with Ashley, and that was years ago. He hasn't evolved very much, I'm afraid."

"Ashley?" I didn't know Gavin even had an ex, didn't think he'd ever been in a serious relationship.

"Sorry. I figured he would have mentioned her in all the time you guys have been spending together lately. Forget I said anything; it's not my place to tell you that story."

"But she's an ex-girlfriend?"

He nodded again. "She was.

"Was it a messy breakup?"

Cooper paused, and the tension in the air seemed to increase exponentially. "No, actually. She passed away a couple of years ago. Unexpectedly."

My stomach twisted into a hard knot.

Chapter Thirty-Two

Emma

"Ready, *chica*?" Bethany said, grinning as I opened my front door.

"You mind coming in for a second? I'm kind of in the middle of something."

And that something was Internet stalking my new boyfriend. Excuse me—my *person*.

"Sure. What's up?" she asked, following me to the kitchen table where my laptop sat.

Ever since the revelation that Cooper let slip, I was obsessed with learning more. Who was Ashley? Was she the reason Gavin was so damaged and fearful about starting a relationship?

"Just doing a little research." I slid into the chair opposite the laptop and resumed my hunt.

Bethany stood behind me, peering over my shoulder. "Is that Gavin?"

I nodded. There was an image of him at a black-tie event standing between Quinn and Cooper. I didn't know why I'd never thought to google him before. This was fascinating.

"Is there a particular reason we're stalking him today rather than eating tacos right now?"

"I learned that Gavin had an ex who passed away suddenly. The tacos can wait," I muttered. This was important. How did she not get that?

"Yes, but half-priced margaritas can't." She tapped the time in the lower left-hand corner of my screen. "Happy hour ends at six."

"Oh, look at this. I think I've found it." I stopped scrolling and enlarged a photo of Gavin with a mystery woman on his arm. She was slender and pretty with long dark hair that fell in a silky wave, and sky-blue eyes so light and piercing, they were almost haunting.

An eerie chill zipped down my spine.

"Holy shit." Bethany leaned closer. "That's her?"

The caption below the photo read SMUT MOGUL GAVIN KINGSLEY OUT FOR AN EVENING WITH HIS LONGTIME GIRLFRIEND, ASHLEY MOORE.

"Uh-huh." I nodded, my words failing me.

"She could be your twin, Emma. I've heard of someone having a type, but that's just creepy."

Creepy didn't even begin to cover it. My throat threatened to close, air become scarce, and the room tilted sideways.

My fingers flying over the keys, I typed her full name into the search bar and hit ENTER.

The first result was a news article about the mysterious death of a model. I clicked on the link. Bethany pulled a chair out from the table and slid in next to me. We both held our breath as I scrolled down so we could read it.

Ashley had been young, only twenty-four. That stuck out to me for some reason. Gavin was thirty-four. I couldn't even imagine not losing my head over a man so commanding and intense at her young age.

Miss Moore was found dead at a residence belonging to the elusive multi-millionaire Gavin Kingsley with ligature marks on her wrists and neck.

Bewildered, I stared at the words on the screen, trying to make sense of them. Gavin had a penchant for rough sex, but surely he wouldn't . . .

Panicked and disturbed, I slammed the laptop closed. I heard Bethany's voice in the distance, calling my name.

"Emma! Are you okay?"

I shook my head. "Give me my phone."

"What does all this mean?" she asked, standing beside me while I dialed and held the phone to my ear.

With shaking hands, I waited, listening to the phone ring once, twice . . .

Pick up. Please, pick up.

Finally. His deep, familiar voice echoed through the speaker.

"Princess. Everything okay?"

"No." My voice broke into a sob. "I need you."

"I'll be right there."

Up Next in the Forbidden Desires Series

Dirty Little Promise

The secret I discovered about sexy multi-millionaire Gavin Kingsley is so big, so daunting, it isn't something I can overcome. I have a decision to make—hear him out and see where things go, or turn to his brother Cooper, who I'm fairly certain is in love with me. But something dark inside of Gavin calls to something dark inside of me. And I'm not willing to just walk away . . . not yet, anyway.

This is the conclusion to Emma Bell's epic love affair with the alpha and enigmatic Kingsley brothers. Secrets will be exposed, sides will be chosen, and nothing will ever be the same.

Also in This Series

Dirty Little Promise

Torrid Little Affair

Tempting Little Tease

Acknowledgments

A massive thank-you to the following people for helping this story come to life:

First, to my amazing publicist and right hand in all the things, Danielle Sanchez. When I mentioned this story idea I had for three brothers who owned an escort agency, and you said, "Ohhh, you should write that next," your enthusiasm was the reason I did.

Author Rachel Brookes, thank you for believing in my alpha asshole brothers, and for loving this story. It means the world.

Thank you to GoodReads diva extraordinaire Sue Bee for taking the time to beta read this book. Your feedback and guidance helped tremendously, and I was so happy when the queen of fictional alpha males told me that I had nailed Gavin, and that his hot and cold personality was perfect.

For Natasha Madison, thank you for loving everything I write.

A huge thank-you to Sarah Hansen for my lovely covers for this series, and to Michelle Tan for designing such beautiful graphics.

To Alyssa Garcia, you deal with my crazy on a daily basis, and I'm so thankful to have you as my executive assistant. It only seemed right to name Gavin's assistant after you.

Thank you to the team at Radish for believing in this story.

Thank you to all the wonderful reviewers, bloggers, librarians, booksellers, and readers who requested early review copies. We were overwhelmed by your excitement for this book.

A huge tackle-hug and a glass of fizzy champagne to all the readers who purchased a copy. You are the reason I get to continue bringing my stories to life, and I truly hope you loved it as much as I did. I cannot wait to bring you more in the story, including more books about all three brothers.

About the Author

A *New York Times*, *Wall Street Journal*, and *USA TODAY* bestselling author of more than two dozen titles, Kendall Ryan has sold over two million books, and her books have been translated into several languages in countries around the world. Her books have also appeared on the *New York Times* and *USA TODAY* bestseller list more than three dozen times. Ryan has been featured in publications such as *USA TODAY*, *Newsweek*, and *In Touch Magazine*. She lives in Texas with her husband and two sons.

Other Books by Kendall Ryan

Unravel Me
Make Me Yours
Working It
Craving Him
All or Nothing
When I Break Series
Filthy Beautiful Lies Series
The Gentleman Mentor
Sinfully Mine
Bait & Switch
Slow & Steady
The Room Mate
The Play Mate
The House Mate
The Bed Mate
The Soul Mate
Hard to Love
Reckless Love
Resisting Her
The Impact of You
Screwed
Monster Prick
The Fix Up
Sexy Stranger

For a complete list of Kendall's books, visit:

http://www.kendallryanbooks.com/all-books/

Made in the USA
Columbia, SC
23 August 2023

22032212R00212